And Kelsey makes Three

(a Galactic Love Store, Book 3)

By

Viola Quincy

And Kelsey Makes Three

Kelsey- My twenty-first birthday should have been a really fun day, instead I dumped my jerk of a boyfriend when I caught him kissing my so-called best friend, and instead I partied with a bunch of handsy sailors. Getting away from them, I drunkenly wandered the waterfront of Liberty Bay, trying to walk off the booze before driving home when I was abducted by these creepy, scrawny aliens. The other ladies and I were rescued by this group of muscle bound alien marines. Who knew that there were so many different types of gorgeous males in the Universe, I was very intrigued by these beautiful men, but the Captain, of the new ship we are on, and his brother are a pair of sticks in the mud, who thwart my attempts to flirt with the plethora of beefcake on this ship. It is weird though, I find them to be the most gorgeous and interesting of all the males. My dreams are all of doing naughty things with them... With both of them...What kind of girl am I?

Tet and Tan - Yes, we are twins with a psychic connection. We have found our mate and it is a big problem for us. Like many species under the Galactic Federation, our species has few females for mating with and, as Acadianans, we hoped to find that special female that would be our mate and fit into our life, but had little hope. Then we met her...a human...One of the females we liberated from the misagian slavers. She is chaos personified and she is creating mayhem among our crew with her antics! How could the gods bring this immature youngling into our lives... though we have been assured she is an adult, which is good, because we both desire her in a way that would be inappropriate if she wasn't of age. Both of us must find a way to tame our mate or we may be forced to never mate,...

This is for a mature audience who like happily ever afters with sexy, big aliens. Themes include a Male/Male/Female relationship, drunkeness, kidnapping, slavery, and much dirty minded smut. NO cheating and no rape :-)

Table of Contents

Trigger Warnings

This story has some stuff that might cause some issues for some. If any of these things cause you problems, this may not be the story for you. Themes include:

- kidnapping and alien abduction are prominent in the story.
- Pregnancy and descriptions of birth.
- Over indulgence of alcohol and drunkeness.
- Sexual situations with aliens and humans.
- Sexual situations that have questionable consent and multiple partners.
- Also, the story includes a bit of trauma response to death.

Dedication

Creating a new story within a world established by prior books can be a bit daunting. There is making sure that your stories mesh and then there is the editing. The editing is a killer. Thanks to my two editors, Mary and Yves. They both read through the rough draft and found all my mistakes. So many mistakes, mostly grammar. I am a comma Queen! So, this book is dedicated to them.

Prologue - Kelsey

Poulsbo, WA present day - I am enjoying a lovely stroll on the shores of Liberty Bay…OK, I'm drunk off my ass and stumbling along, while the geoducks[1] spit streams of salty water up my skirt, causing me to squeal. Don't worry, it's 3 AM and almost all the lights from the houses and buildings are off. I am walking on the sand near the waterfront park and almost to the end of the beachfront when I started getting cold and thought I should walk back to my car. It is down at the bar on Front Street where I had been partying. The tide is coming in and in my drunken haze I realize I need to get back to the walking path.

Why am I so drunk? Don't judge, but it's my 21st birthday and I was going to party. But then, I caught my asshole now former boyfriend making out with my now former best friend. What the hell? His excuse? I flirt too much and Carissa was just soothing his pride. I said fuck him and his lying and cheating ways. Oh, and trying to gaslight me?…Yeah, fuck that, too. I love flirting and the attention that good looking men give me. Alright, I need the attention of good-looking men. But that is its own issue. If Larson had wanted an open relationship, then all he needed to do was ask me and I would have probably agreed, I am not that stuck on monogamy, but he was all like, "You are my one and only."

---

[1] Geoducks (pronounced GOO-eeducks} – are a very large saltwater clam renowned for its obscene looks and spitting at the unwary. Found mostly in the Puget Sound).

So...OK...but I wanted to dance and he never does. Like the old song says, I may dance with a lot of guys, but I never forgot who I was going home with. And he cheated with my best friend! He had his hand on her boobs and neither of them were THAT drunk. We had been at that club for only an hour or, maybe, an hour and a half. Anyway, I left and came to this bar in downtown Poulsbo, WA.

So, there I was, no boyfriend or bestie to celebrate with. I just started talking to every good looker and got several to buy me a drink. I had to use my slippery, girly tricks to get away from a few sailors from NSB Bangor, thought I would go down on them for a frothy, boozy drink, but no thank you... Not happening. I quit doing that when Larson said he wouldn't go down on me because it wasn't "sanitary" ...really? Well then, I guess he didn't want to have that special loving for Mr. Happy, because he wasn't that good in bed. Truly, I don't think he knew that there was this thing called a "clit". All he knew is stick his rod into my hole, pump a few times, grunt, and say, "Ah Babe, that was so good for me, how about for you?" To which, I usually lied to save his ego. He seemed to be really good boyfriend material. He took me out to good restaurants, at first. He would compliment me and tell me I was pretty every day, for the first few weeks. We had been dating for five months and I was thinking that he might be "the one", but I may have been fooling myself. Really, he was starting to bore me, but he had been hinting that maybe we should think of a more serious relationship. I was intrigued. I had never dated for longer than a few weeks before I found myself telling the nice guy that I didn't think it was going to work out. So, five months was a lifetime for me… Now, I am glad I was done with Larson, his flat ass, stupid jokes and greasy hair… OK, that may be the booze talking.

I just turned 21 and it was my first time legally drinking hard liquors. I had had the occasional glass of wine… Grandmama said it was important that ladies be able to drink fine wine with their meals and so when I turned 16, my training began. I could tell with a taste the brand, year, and grape. It was OK but I wasn't a big wine drinker, especially after trying a Jager shot at a Frat party over at UW.

While I had tasted different beverages at parties throughout Puget Sound, I never had as much as I had had this particular night. Those sailors…Oh, excuse me, submariners, are really fun to party with at this bar on the waterfront in Poulsbo. But when last call came, I didn't want to go home with any of the men that were there. I firmly told them I was going to go meet my friends at the beach and thanks for the great night. A few tried, but I was able to move out without them.

So, here I am wandering the waterfront, almost *in* the water. I was cutting through the trees when I feel a prick on the neck… *"What the Fuck?"*… I howl as I turn to see a creepy looking guy looking at me then I began to collapse and my world goes black.

Chapter One - Tet

My twin and I are becoming more frustrated with the Marine Commander that the Galactic Federation has placed on our ship. It was bad enough that we were close to the border of an unauthorized, highly, illegal solar system. My orders are to let Commander Max determine the course of our destination. The Caeterin commander is driving us crazy with his demands to go to this star system, now head that way. He couldn't make up his mind, but then he saw the Misagian ship and we were off. The chase was Tan and my department while Commander Max and his marines boarded the enemy ship.

As they boarded, we did not realize that we would have to scramble ships to go after the escape pods. Max is cagey like that. Never telling us what the plan was. However, we got most of them, but several escaped us. Next thing Tan and I know, we are trying to find accommodations for several females... *Human females...* The Misagians were shipping them to a remote outpost to sell as slaves.

The females will have to stay onboard the *Patience* for the time being. We can not just send them back to C-348 or as Max says the humans refer to it "Earth". Federation laws state that Earth is a primitive world not ready for the technology of the Galactic Federation. However, human females have become sought after in the illegal slavery markets on the outskirts of Federation space. The council has stated that too many human females are being found in Federation space and we needed to stop those who are violating many of the Galactic Federation's laws to enslave humans. We needed to find out who is funding these raids to C-348 and stop the abductions.

The chime to my conference room goes off. When Commander Max enters, he places his left fist to his chest in respectful salute to me then a nod to my twin. "Sir, the females are all bunked down in the marine quarters. My males were happy to accommodate them." I give Max a curt nod as I try not to laugh at my brothers...*I am so sure they are happy. Nine females all together.*

"At least, you did not disrupt the operation the ship further." I growl. "You will be fully responsible for these females while they are on my ship."

"Yes, sir." He displays confidence "These human females seem like reasonable beings and we rescued them from the Misagian slavers. I am sure they will be no trouble, sir."

"We will see." I acknowledge, *I am so sure they will be no trouble at all. After all, it isn't like humans are not gaining a troublesome reputation.* A snort coming from Tan. I have to be more circumspect.

"You will need to let them know that while we will be docking at the Council's station, they will not be able to leave. There have been some abductions of freed humans on Federation space stations in the last few hours. The slavers are getting bold. The council feels that we would do best to keep these females on board until the criminals behind their abductions are stopped or the females are found a secure place to be deposited."

"Sir, that could take years." I nod, glad that the commander understands the severity of this situation.

"Yes, Commander, and your Marines will be expected to stay on board until this is resolved to help with the females." I give him a tight smile.

"Sir, if I may, the females are currently living practically on top of each other in an enlisted bunk. For a few days or weeks this would be fine, but we could be talking months. Is there a way we can spread them out amongst the crew quarters." he suggests, "There are only seven who need to be placed in other bunks. We can put three in the Marine barracks and then move two each in two cabins within your officer space." He looks hopeful but I have questions.

He has got a point there, Tet. My brother says in our own manner. *I have heard he has housed two of the females; a mother and child.*

"Are there not nine females?" I ask.

"Yes, sir. There are, but two of the females are a mother and her youngling." He confirms, "I have given them my cabin, so they have the needed space. The child is young if a tad precocious." There is a strange aura coming from him, I sense that there is more…

"In your cabin? Is that appropriate, Commander?" I query. I feel concern coming from him, like he is pondering strong thoughts.

"I think in this case, it is. For the time being, I am staying with my executive officer, Lt. Commander B'Jox." I look at my brother, *Do you feel that, Tan?*

Indeed, I think this male is smitten with the human female."

"Somehow, I think you are not telling me the whole truth, Max. What is going on with you and that female?" I say. We look at him pointedly

"Nothing, Sir," My eyebrows raise at that "At least, not yet." He hesitates.

"Go on…" I really want to hear this. My brother agrees.

"Well, Sir. I suspect she is my true mate." *His true mate?* Tan is shocked.

"You do? How did you come to this conclusion, Commander?" Tan asks in his rough voice.

"My beast goes crazy in the mother's presence, sir. I will need to get really close to her and scent her to confirm this suspicion. However, I have very serious feelings for her and the child, like it is my duty… and my honor to protect them both." *He is so earnest, Brother. I fear he truly has found his mate.* My brother is amused.

"Then go scent her and take her as your mate!" I am happy to let the commander have his mate. So many of us will not have this wonderful gift. *a true gift*, my brother echoes.

"Sir, in my dealings with humans, particularly, Admiral Car'Athos's mate, Elizabeth, I have found that they are not used to having strange males scent them." He explains, "As I have just met this human, I will need to… I believe the word is 'court' her, before she will let me get close enough to verify that she is my true mate."

"I am concerned, Max, that these females will prove troublesome. If nothing else, having them all over the ship may encourage my males to be distracted by their very presence." Tan states, but to me,

We may need to contain the females. If he is mated to one of these females what of others? This could cause chaos

I agree. "The fewer places where they can encounter the males on my ship the more stability in my crew. Do you understand, Commander Max?"

"Yes, sir.," He states.

"Very well, you can let them bunk in three of the lesser officer cabins, move those officers into your extra crew bunks, and you will show the females the most private route to the officer's mess. I will not have them trapsing all over my ship. Is that understood?"

They shouldn't even be on a ship. My brother says to me.

You may be correct but we have no choice. Besides there is more to think of at this time than what we want to do. I continue to look at the commander.

"Yes, sir." He salutes and makes his way to the exit

"And Max?" I stop him as a solution may present itself.

"Yes, Captain?"

"One last thing. Find out if that female is your mate and deal with it." I smile at him. "We may need to see all these females mated to protect them."

"Yes Sir! I will work towards this goal." Another salute and he exits.

You sure there is no way we can get rid of them. My twin muses. *I feel a sense of unease with having all these females on board.*

I feel it too, I agree with him, *There is something different happening. It is like our destiny is entwined with this mission…with these humans.*

Maybe we should house the females in the brig and reduce the number of crew members who are exposed to their influence. I chuckle.

You haven't even met a human and you want to imprison all the females.

Tet, I have heard of the trouble that human females have caused in some of the space stations. According to my sources, they are chaotic. They don't approach any situation with logic and reason. Tan looked and felt truly apprehensive. *I see no good coming from these females. They will disrupt life on our ship.* Tan has always been a worrier.

If it is our destiny, there is nothing we can do to prevent it .I think we will go with the plan in motion and see where fate takes us," I feel his frustration but it cannot be helped. *"Let's head to the mess and see what they have cooked up. We missed the Mid-shift meal.*

Yes, captain! Tan responds, with a salute, his fist on his chest.

You know how I hate when you do that. I grumble. Tan just laughs. I slap him on the back of the head. As I head to the panel on the door and press it to open the doorway, he shakes his head and chuckles.

You will feel better after we eat.

Chapter Two – Kelsey

Well, this sucks. Not only did I get abducted on my birthday and found myself on an alien starship with no hope of ever going home, but I can't even get off this stupid ship until they figure out how to stop the assholes from abducting human women. Maybe then I can figure out my new life.

I liked my old one. I mean, it wasn't perfect, but I was doing alright. I have a double BS in astronomy and astrophysics, and just one more semester to my masters. I like physics and astronomy; my mathematical skills are amazing. I would have gone on to get a honors fellowship to help pay for my doctorate, but, well, an alien abduction put a stop to that idea.

The party scene in the Puget Sound area wasn't too bad. I also like to party and have a good time. Not a complete nerd, really. Besides, my degree wasn't something I mentioned to my dates. Heck, even Larson didn't know what I was studying. Ya know, I don't think he even asked. Now, that I think of it, he probably thought I was a Liberal Arts major…or…Oh, wait…*The asshole thought I was a nursing student*…I see it now. Every fricken cut or scrape, every time he had the sniffles… he was like, "Babe, you take care of me so well." And now, I see it. Dang, I am an idiot…but an idiot who could join MENSA if I wanted to…and I don't… Too many boys who think they are the smartest kids in the room… *OK they are*…but they don't have to act like that makes them superior to average people. You know folks that listen to pop music, not Mozart or like watching TV shows that aren't on PBS or Nat Geo. They used to like the History Channel, but the more interesting shows weren't "real history"…Hey, *Pawn Stars* always had some interesting tidbits about the artifacts brought in.

So, anyway, not my scene. I like dumb TV shows and pop culture. I like reading romance novels where the male characters are so the opposite of the guys I meet. I especially, like monsters and big horny aliens…yeah, yeah, both meanings. I am not a victim of virginity. Unlike my companion, Victoria. She's kind of nice. Has that East Coast attitude that is almost as bad as the Californians. You know, the "we are the center of the cultural world". OK, they have a lot going on, but Western Washington is beautiful and we have real mountains. Yeah, it is cloudy and drizzly most of the year, however our spring gardens are amazing. Not that I garden…Well, Victoria, the virgin, is all freaked out. See she is a good Puerto Rican Catholic girl from New York. So good, she was attending a Catholic Young Adult retreat in California when she was abducted. Evidently, the West Coast Catholics were more morally loose than her New York Catholics and it was freaking her out, so she went into the woods to seek solitude and pray for their souls…or something like that. She was telling me all about how she thought about being a nun but realized that she really wanted to be a mom and raise several kids, maybe even adopting some. She is twenty four and still not married, I thought that would be an easy for someone as pretty as her. Like me she has a few too many curves, but I heard Hispanic guys dug a little more cushion for the pushin'. "So why aren't you married?" I just have to ask.

"I thought that I would find a Catholic man of similar background, but I don't know what happened," She says as we walked down a hallway towards the officers' mess…I don't know why they called it that, but it is where we go to eat…and I am hungry…So, I spent most of the stroll trying to pay attention. Victoria was going on about her big crush on of all things a visiting priest from Columbia, "And no other man could compare to Father Antonio. I was hoping that getting out of my parish and meeting other young Catholics might help but then they were so different. Most were really young… and girls. They were more interested in their phones than trying to build their faith. The speakers were amazing. Sister Catherine was discussing the way women in the Church needed to be the foundation in our relationships, but…"

I'm really hungry and getting bored, "But what are you going to do now that we are in space. You think there is a Catholic alien out here?"

"That is what I am worried about. If I can't go home to Earth, will I be able to ever marry?" She looks really shook by that realization.

"Hey, in my romance novels, there are all kinds of aliens!" I assure her, "Just because they may not be Catholic,

God maybe has a plan for you to find that guy who can have a similar philosophy," I turn fully towards her, walking backwards, and my wild child decides to add, "I have decided that I am going to have a reverse harem! Two or three of these hunky males and all the se…" Bump! Right into a wall of muscles.

Slowly, I turn and come face to face with not one but two huge muscular chests. I heard Victoria gasp, and my eyes start to rise up to the most beautiful faces I had ever seen. They are identical. Tall, so tall. I am five ten, so pretty used to being close to the same height as most of the men I met. However, these two are a good foot and a half taller than me. They look like a pair of dark elves with pointed ears complete with piercings down one side. Their skin is shiny and black as night Their hair is white as snow though only one has the long locks expected of those fabled Tolkien creatures. The other's is shorn in a military cut…Well, they are military right?…We are on a military ship, after all. *Yeah, but they are looking down those beautiful straight noses at you, girl. Better think quick…*

"Oh, hey there," I greet the elven gods with a cheeky grin, "Sorry, I wasn't paying attention"

"We could see that, female," the one with the long hair says. His voice is sexy, low but I could hear a bit of a sneer in his growly voice. Well, I won't be turned off by that.

"You two look like twins or is this an all aliens look alike." I continue to smile cheerily at the dour hunks. Victoria was picking at my shirt, trying to hide from the aliens while trying to get me moving.

"We are twins, female, and you are the aliens. We belong here." Mister Military Cut growls, "You should watch where you are going when on our ship."

I put on my best batty blonde big eyes, "Your ship, huh? Do you like own it?"

"I am the captain and my brother is our first officer." I am beginning to feel like a bit of a bug as these males just stand there studying me, "If you will excuse us, female. We are needed in the bridge."

"My name is Kelsey, Captain? You didn't give your name." I query giving my eyes a few bats.

"Not that it matters, *Kel – see*, but I am Captain Tet Bl'Wski and this is my twin and first officer Commander Tan Bl'Wski, he nods at his name, "You females should stay to your rooms or the officer's mess. We do not need you affecting operations of this vessel. Please discuss any needs with the Marine Commander Max. He is in charge of you."

"Aye Aye, Captain," I say with a smart military salute. The males just look at me like I am crazy… "Context is everything, guys, excuse us."

I push my hands between them to make a path, for Victoria and I, by laying my hands on their upper arms and with a slight push. There was a little spark when my hands slipped and touched a bit of skin under the short sleeves of their uniforms.

As I move past, the males are looking at each other with a weird look. I probably shouldn't have touched them, wondering if I broke some taboo, but I was really glad I did. Those biceps were some really prime specimens. Too bad they are attached to such stuffed shirts. Victoria and I walked down the hall. Hoping that was the last encounter with those males… they are gorgeous…Nope, they are assholes and I am done trying to attract assholes. I am on a ship full of males, I will find my entertainment without those two…*but why did I want to get a second touch?*… I must be hungry…That is all this is. I am hungry. I hurry Victoria along to the mess. Dinner was waiting.

Chapter Three – Tan

As we stood in the hallway, watching the two females walk down the hall, we are in stunned silence. We had been having dinner when a call came from the bridge. The human bounced off of us, because she was walking backwards. Very irrational. But when she touched us…

You felt that, didn't you? I know he had, but I needed to confirm this.

Yes, I felt it. I am not sure how I feel about this. Tet looks at his forearm… and there it is…I look at mine…the mating marks are faint but there.

How could this be? She is…

I know. But, you have to admit, she is magnificent in her chaos. There is a slight mystified smile on Tet mouth. *What do we do about this?*

What can we do? I reply, *The gods have sent us our mate, but she is a whirlwind of mayhem. We are command officers of the Galactic Federation. How are we going to control that female…our …mate.*

We will be thankful for we have …what many do not. We have a mate, Tan reminds me of our good luck, but I am not so sure. *We will tell her after her meal and move her into our cabin right away. In fact,* He hits his com…

What are you doing? I ask.

I am contacting, Ensign Tarvek. He states. *He will move her possessions to our cabin while she is eating.*

I do not think you should assume that she wants to be moved. I can see the issues with this plan, *Commander Max even said that humans do not mate like others in the Galaxy.*

Tet was not going to be dissuade. *Max isn't any more clued in as we are. I am the captain of the Patience. She is our mate. The sooner she excepts that the sooner we can **train** her to be our perfect female.* I have a bad feeling about this, but my brother is determined to follow this path.

We have work to do. Let's not get distracted at this time. We will work on this tomorrow. I need to get away from the scent of her. I take a deep breath and close my eyes. I can't believe how much I just want to follow that female.

I feel the same way, Brother. We will deal with this later. As we continue down the hall.

The reason Tet is the captain is because he is the more sociable and practical of the two of us. I am the more logical and have a need for order. I rarely speak unless I see a need to and I can't just have Tet relay my thoughts in the moment. But we are a team. What worries me is how that female will fit into our comfortable and well ordered lives. She looks and acts like a youngling. *Do you think she is even old enough to be a mate?* I ask Tet.

How should I know? I do not know anything more about humans than you do. I look at my brother with a worried frown. We are only 74, still in the prime of our lives, given our species has a life expectancy of 200, but to be mated to a youngling. That would not be acceptable. Not that being mated to that human is. What will we do?

Chapter Four -Tet

My brother and I walk into the Officers Mess, to find our mate surrounded by several of our officers. All of them looking at her with adoration. *This is not acceptable. My brother feels agitated.*

I know. We may need to move her to our room now and have her meals brought to her until we have claimed her.

As all of the officers notice us…well, me… they all pop to a standing attention. Commander Max moves towards us with two human females beside him. He salutes then moves the older human female forward. She is a bit taller than the tiny human that is our mate. But even she is tiny compared to the males of this ship.

"Captain Bl'Wski…Commander Bl'Wski, May I present Maryellen Bishop and her daughter, 'Jaycee'"

The youngling speaks. "'Mander is gonna be my daddy!"

The older female grabs her and makes a shushing sound. *It seems the Marine Commander has been successful.* My brother is still agitated, I assume due to our mate being in the room. I smile as I say out loud, "I would hope so, youngling. Commander Max would be a good protector. That is what you females will all need as there is a lot of danger out there. You …humans…are small and weak. This part of the Universe has too many who prey on those who are weaker."

"Dude!" Our mate calls out as she moves toward us, "Don't be scaring that child! We women will happily protect this child! She is just a little kid, you big jerk." Suddenly, she is right in front of me. *What is she doing? Doesn't she have any discipline?* My brother is more upset than I have ever seen him. *Tan, you need to calm down!* I am in charge and will contain this.

"Female! Control yourself. I merely state the truth." I can't let this outburst continue. However, I quickly realize that I need to address all the humans. "You need to realize that you all will be better off if you find a mate to protect you!" *It is the most logical solution,* Tan agrees.

"We don't need some males trying to control us!" Another human adds her unruly voice. This one has a skin color that is more a light brown than the pinkish color of our own mate.

"I refuse to mate with an alien!" Now, a human with skin that, while not as dark as Tan and mine, is much darker than all the other women save one.

The crew do not like what is happening. We need to stop this now, my brother! Tan is right, the crew are looking upset by these statements.

Maybe humans ARE more chaotic than we thought. Tan's confusion and anger is rising as Kelsey moves in front him. She looks glorious with her blue eyes spitting fire and her hands fisted on her full hips. Hips that I desire under me as I … No, I can't be distracted by her.

The lovely mate of Commander Max cuts in, "Kelsey, why don't you go finish your breakfast. Ladies, I am sure that Captain

Bl'Wski has no intention of forcing a mating on any of you. Do you, Captain?" Well, not force no… This would be a bad thing.

"No, of course not," I assure her. "It seems I may have offended you females with my practical suggestion." Kelsey snorts. Tan and I look at her. I feel Tan's emotions rising. He stares at the little firebrand. This is not normal for him, but our mate doesn't appear aware of her effect on him…on us.

"I am sure that there are cultural misunderstandings on all our parts." Max's human says soothingly.

"Commander Max, it seems you have been blessed with a wise female to be your mate," Tan states in his soft voice, *I wish the same could be said of our mate. This is a female that would be appropriate for Akkadianans of our rank and status.*

She is Max's not ours. The Universe has a reason for this. I do not have a clue why we are "gifted" with the beautiful, but ill-disciplined female but she is ours and I hope I figure this all out before we are overwhelmed by this disorder.

"I am, but only if she will accept my claim." I can see that Max is so proud of his lovely mate. "She is spectacular and she brings with her this amazing youngling, Jaycee."

"Mommy. I like 'Mander kitty man. I want him for my daddy. Please." The human looks a tad uncomfortable. Maybe Commander Max isn't having as easy a time. Tan and I glance at each other in understanding.

"Baby, I need to discuss this with Rin'On. There is a lot to consider." The human is a bit uncertain. "Now, Missy. Go finish your breakfast." The youngling runs to the table, climbs into the big chair, and begins eating.

"Now back to our discussion," Maryellen… that's her name… says, "I am sure the ladies would all like to know what is going on and what our options are. Rin'On, I mean Commander Max, has said that we will be living on this ship for the foreseeable future?"

"Yes, that is true, Lady Maryellen." I respond.

"Just Maryellen is fine. The situation is just not acceptable." She states. "I realize that you don't have much say in this, as it came down the command chain, I assume?" *She is familiar with military structure and bureaucracy,*. I say to my brother.

Again, why didn't the Universe choose this female for us? He replies.

Are you really attracted to her? I know the answer to this, but I need him to see this.

She is beautiful and wise but no, Kelsey is what my body wants… His eyes traverse the curves of our mate.

"That is correct." I nod, "The Council for the Galactic Federation has said we must keep you as comfortable as possible, but in the interest of keeping you safe from the criminal elements that have brazenly entered Federation space to kidnap the few humans there are from our space stations and colonies, you need to stay aboard The Patience."

"You can see our position, can't you," She says in a pleasant voice, that bely the turmoil I feel from her. "Except for my little girl, all of us humans are women, adults on our world." *That is a relief, brother! Our mate may be immature, but she is an adult.* Tan reflects our mutual relief "We are not used to being pinned up. We need things…personal things, that I doubt a ship crewed solely by military males is going to have…"

"I bet you don't even carry tampons or pads for when Aunt Flo comes a-callin', do you Captain." Kelsey says from behind Maryellen.

What is she talking about?

I have no idea. Who is this Aunt Flo?

Maryellen grabs her hand and squeezes it in a maneuver to quiet her while quickly saying, and appears to calm her. "There is, also, the matter of I am a mother with a child that should have space to run and play. Also, she needs her education, what does your Galactic Council plan to do about that?"

My brother and I look at each other for a moment. *She is making some good points.*

How do we care for the humans when we can't understand their needs? Tan replies.

We need to communicate and learn, that much I know. As I look back to the females.

"We will need to consult with the Council," I begin, "Who is this Aunt Flo? If she is on Earth, there is nothing we can do for her." All the females start chuckling.

What's so funny?

I do not know.

"It's our period…our menses…our cycle," Kelsey says, "We bleeeeeddd from our uteruses for one week a month, unless we are pregnant." My eyes widen. Tan is horrified.

We will need to keep our mate breeding, so we do not experience this. It sounds dangerous!

"Which I am not sure being in this part of the Universe would be good for childrearing." She continues. Neither of us like that statement, "Who to teach these folks about human anatomy?"

"I guess I could," Says the other dark skinned female.

Humans come in such a range of skin colors. Fascinating, isn't it? I look at my brother as she continues.

"I was in my third year of residency at Portland's OHSU. While I can only do so much, I could work with your doctors to get them familiar with human anatomy." *Another useful female. Very good.*

"Our medics would appreciate that, I am sure, Female." I am still a bit confused but this seems a good plan for now, "I will talk to our chief medic and see when he has a moment to meet with you."

"Oh, Michelle, that would be great!" Maryellen exclaims, "You could still continue on your career path."

"In a way," She says, "I was hoping to transfer to a pediatric surgery rotation, if one opened up, but I guess it will be good to be a GP for those humans who need medical care."

"Well, let's discuss what skills we have, so Captain Bl'Wski and his first officer can find us gainful employment." She gestures to the tables.

"Female, while I am pleased that some of you have skills that will prove useful," I begin, "I worry that without mates, you will be targets."

"Of all the misogynistic crap!" Kelsey exclaims, "We are adult women. We can take care of ourselves. I appreciate the rescue by Commander Max and his men, but the idea of sitting back and being the little woman so some entitled, drooling Neanderthal is just not in the cards. We need to have purpose beyond being housewives."

"Silence, female!" Tan shouts. I am not the only one that is stunned by his outburst. stuns everyone by his outburst. Tan takes Kelsey by the back of her neck, holding in a firm, yet gentle grip, forcing her to look into his eyes, "You will all have mates, because when you are properly mated you will have no value to the slavers."

"Commander? I think you are being a bit harsh." Max's female tries to calm the situation as several of the females had risen from the tables.

"She must learn her place on this ship and the Universe." He grits out of his teeth. Kelsey looks confused then defiance crosses our mates face and radiates from her. Maryellen tries to remove Kelsey from Tan's grip. His hand opens quickly, as if he was shocked that he was holding her.

Chaos! She is pure chaos. I feel Tan's emotions are swirling.

Brother, calm yourself. It will be solved.

"Hey," The human whispers to our mate, "if you are done with your breakfast, you might want to go back to your cabin for a bit. Hmmm."

"I will just go sit with the fellas over there and get something." She looks at Tan. I feel a touch of fear and... desire?

"The female will sit between the captain and I." Tan states powerfully.

"But I don't want to sit with you, commander." Kelsey begins, "After how you manhandled me. What makes you think I want anything to do with you?" He leans over and whispers in her ear. *You want the discipline, my beauty, I feel your desire.* I know he tells our mate.

Her eyes widen, her face becomes reddened and her arm comes up... but she is unable to complete the strike, because in a move that is lightning fast Tan has grasped her wrist and pulls her into his arms.

"I said nothing untrue and you will not strike me for stating the truth." Tan then picks her up and slings her over his shoulder. He leaves the mess with a screeching Kelsey.

Tan! What are you doing?

Follow me and find out. I will tame this female! She is our mate and needs discipline!

Um… I will need to see to this," I begin, "Major Vret! Please have our usual first meal delivered to my quarters. "Females, please think on what I have said. I bid you good day.", and I am out the door chasing after my brother and mate.

Chapter Five – Kelsey

Y ou asshole!" I scream into the broad back of Commander Tan Bl'Wski, my fists beating uselessly against those solid muscles, "Put me the fuck down!"

ᴴᵉ just slams his palm down on my ass. "Female! Control yourself and quit screeching like schrihak."

I scream at the pain on my butt and hit him again. I know that it hurts me more than him, but whatever his plan for me is, I am not going to let him think I fear him… I am a little fearful …but not that much. Something tells me he wouldn't seriously hurt me. I think I just pushed his buttons a bit too far. He needed shaking up, I bet. His reaction shows he isn't used to being challenged.

"Where are you taking me?" I ask.

"Our cabin, Mate." He replies in that beautiful, growly baritone.

"Wh…What are you talking about?" Our cabin? he says…Mate? He called me…Mate?!? "Oh no! I am not your mate!" I will not let him mate me…though he does have a beautiful butt that I get a full view from this angle. "I am too much for any one male. Nope. Not a mate."

He turns into a large door that opens into a large "living room" space when he hefts me back up and gently deposits me on a soft couch. "Then it is a good thing The Universe gave you to my brother and I. Two male Akkadianans. Not that I am pleased with the situation."

I look at him with trepidation. "What do you mean 'gave'. I am not a gift."

"No…you are a curse." He stomps to the other side of the cabin, as if he needs to put space between us. "I do not know why we are cursed with a mate who has no discipline, no control!" He seems to be so upset by this, like I am not upset with him, "But all I want to do right now is fuck you until you are too tired to move, let alone cause havoc!" …Um, daaaammmmn, that sounds really…Nope, not going there… however, the thought still leaves my panties dripping with anticipation.

"You didn't choose me to be your mate?" I ask hesitantly. Not really wanting to know the answer.

"Why would I, a commander of the Galactic Federation, chose a chaotic, ill-disciplined female to be my mate!" he pulls up his sleeve and I see the swirling marks on his arm.

"Wow, cool tattoo." I say flippantly to hide my horror of realizing this man…male…isn't interested in me as me, but because universal force…probably the Dark Side, am I right?…has said that he is stuck with me.

"That is NOT a tattoo, whatever that is! Those are my mating marks that started growing up my arm when you touched Tet and I yesterday!" He seems agitated…OK, he has been agitated as long as I have known him.

"Mating marks?" I question, "What are they?" I think I know but I want him to explain. However, we are interrupted as the captain walks into the room. He looks at both of us. Then at his brother. I can feel them having an intense conversation, but I can't hear them. Not acceptable. I will not be ignored.

"Yo dudes! What are you saying to each other?" I say a little louder than I intended, but they need to talk to me.

"I was just reminding my brother that his behavior was not appropriate." Tet looks at me and before I can say a thing, he points at me, "And neither was yours!" I am a bit shocked.

"I was merely sticking up for the women on your ship!" I stand up. "I am going back to my cabin! I don't need to deal with either of you." But before I can go two steps both Tet and Tan are in front of me, blocking my way.

"You are our mate and this is where you will stay until we say you can leave." Tet is almost as firm as Tan in his declaration.

"Mate, schmate…I am not staying here with you two assholes!" I try to move past the pair, but neither is budging.

"Little female, you must accept us as your mates." Tan is suddenly sounding like the reasonable one, after all that chest thumping of his. He gently explains, "If you let us claim you, you will be safe from the slavers. Mates cannot be separated ever."

"Oh, is it illegal to separate mates?" I add a touch of sarcasm to my statement, "Like criminals worry about what is legal or illegal."

"Criminals only do what serves them and a dead slave holds no profits." He states.

"What the Hell? Are you saying if I am mated and they take me, I will die?" I can feel my eyes widening.

"If you are mated to us, we will have to be dead before they can take you," Tet chimes in, "And unless you bear our younglings, you will not survive the tear in our connection. Even with younglings to care for, there is no guarantee that you wouldn't waste away."

"OK, this whole I will die when you die business isn't a selling point, right? I mean I am only 21 and you both are what 35…40? I don't want to die twenty to twenty-five years younger than my lifespan." The males look at each other with a smirk then a guffaw.

"Wait, what's so funny?" I ask.

Tan asks me a question: "What is the average lifespan of a human?"

"I guess, around eighty to eighty-five years." I answer, "With the right genetics and lifestyle humans have been known to live over a hundred years or solar rotations…whatever you call them."

"Hmmm." Tet looks at Tan then back to me. "What if I told you that our species lives well over two hundred years on average? My brother and I have lived only seventy-two- point-one of your years." I am amazed.

"OK, so when I die, you will be a hundred years too young by your standards. You can see why this isn't a good set up, right?"

"Actually, upon claiming the exchange of lifeforce will lengthen your life to match ours." Tet seems confident that I will see this whole claiming thing as a good thing. I am still not sure.

"What does this 'exchange of lifeforce' look like?" I query.

"We, my brother and I, will take you as our ancestors have."
He moves closer to me, until he is almost a breath away, towering
over me. I lookup, up, up into his glowing eyes. I try to step back,
but I am stopped, bumping into that hard chest of Tan. He had
quietly moved behind me. I felt so small and dainty between the two
massive chests. I gulp. I should really be intimidated, but all I want
to do is touch those massive chests.

"A..and, um, how was that?" I want to be sure. No
assumptions here…you just want him to talk dirty to you… Yeah
…OK… ya got me there… Something about these two males really
turns me on. I didn't know I was into this. I never saw me as living a
polyamorous lifestyle, but right now, I am really into the twins and I
want both of them. Right now...

Chapter Six - Tan

When Tet stalked into the room, he was upset.

Why did you do that? Now, they think we are insane! They do not know that she is our mate. I stand there looking at our mate.

It doesn't matter what they think, she is our mate and I needed to get her out of there. I needed to talk to her alone. I needed to be with just her, but Tet does not need to know that.

"Yo dudes! What are you saying to each other?" Kelsey calls out.

Our mate doesn't like to be ignored. Tet looks at me, then back to her.

No, she doesn't. I agree, my eyes move to her.

"I was just reminding *my* brother that his behavior was not appropriate." Tet turns to Kelsey "*And* neither was yours!"

"I was merely sticking up for the women on your ship!" She stands up. "I am going back to my cabin! I don't need to deal with either of you." Tet and I block her quickly.

"You are our mate and this is where you will stay until we say you can leave." Tet is almost as firm as I would be. We can feel her while we tower over her. She isn't frightened by us. In fact, what we feel from her is making both of us uncomfortable, as we feel her attraction to us.

She cannot leave our cabin until she is claimed. I support Tet in this.

"Mate, schmate…I am not staying here with you two assholes!" We do not let her move.

"Little female, you must accept us as your mates." I explain to her. "If you let us claim you, you will be safe from the slavers. Mates cannot be separated ever."

"Oh, is it illegal to separate mates." I catch sarcasm in her statement. "Like criminals worry about what is legal or illegal."

"Criminals only do what serves them and a dead slave holds no profits." I remind her.

"What the Hell? Are you saying if I am mated and they take me, I will die?" Her eyes widen.

"If you are mated to us, we will have to be dead before they can take you," Tet tells her. "And unless you bear our younglings, you will not survive the tear in our connection. Even with younglings to care for, there is no guarantee that you wouldn't waste away."

"OK, this whole I will die when you die business isn't a selling point, right? I mean I am only 21 and you both are what 35…40? I don't want to die twenty to twenty-five years younger than my lifespan." Tet and I look at each other, with a smirk and a chuckle.

She doesn't understand much about us, does she? I tell Tan.

"Wait, what's so funny?" she asks.

"What is the average lifespan of a human." I ask her.

"I guess, around eighty to eighty-five years," she answers.

"With the right genetics and lifestyle humans have been known to live over a hundred years or solar rotations…whatever you call them."

"Hmmm." Tet looks at me.

Her species has a short lifespan? We look back to her and Tet continues.

"What if I told you that our species lives well over two hundred years on average? My brother and I have lived only seventy-two-point-one of your years." I am amazed.

"OK, so when I die, you will be a hundred years too young by your standards. You can see why this isn't a good set up, right?"

"Actually, upon claiming the exchange of lifeforce will lengthen your life to match ours." Tet informs Kelsey.

She will understand that this will benefit her. My brother and I are confident of this.

Damn, she is beautiful and fits so well between us, Tet says.

Yes, she does, but there is still a lot she needs to understand. I remind him.

"What does this 'exchange of lifeforce' look like?" She queries.

"We, my brother and I, will take you as our ancestors have." Tet moves closer to her, until he is almost a breath away. She moves back, bumping into my chest. My cock is straining my trousers, as I just want her to rub that perfect ass against me.

"A..and, um, how was that?" I can sense her need for us.

Should we show her? Tet asks.

She wants us as much as we want her, but I do not think it would be advisable. I try to think about our ship's needs. *She must be willing to change! We can't let our cocks rule over our crew's needs.*

Tet puts his hands on her waist, as I take her upper arms. We feel a need to touch her. Then Tet begins to explain the claiming, bending down to her ear and softly says "The claiming will take place with both Tan and I stroking you, like this." His right hand strokes her cheek, and down her neck. I begin to stroke her other cheek as I move forward following Tet's path on the opposite, until both of us have nestled our hands under the soft mounds that fill our hands with such a wonderous weight.

I want to strip her of these coverings. I want to know how these beautiful mounds feel, Tet tells me.

I do too, but we need to be careful. We cannot afford to let her drag us into her chaos.

"Then we will taste you all over." Both of us, begin to nibble on her ear and along her neck. Her eyes close as a look of ecstasy comes over her face. This encourages us to nibble down her neck. Licking her collarbone.

She tastes wonderful. Tet is as enthralled as I am.

We should stop this. It feels too good, I respond. Tet continues to explain the claiming.

"We will then penetrate your wet cunt together and spill our seed into your womb as we come at the same time." Our hands rub down her clothed body. Both of my hands rubbing and squeezing her magnificent breasts. Tet's hands rubbed her cunt through her clothes.

She is so wet for us, Brother. Tet muses as he continues to pleasure our mate through the fabric. She begins to make sweet little noises that go straight to my cock.

"B…b…both of you?" She is panting and moving her hips in rhythm of Tet's hand.

"Yes, my mate. Both of us. We cannot breed you unless both of us fuck your sweet little cunt as one." I growl at her with my need to taste more of her. Her lips open for us as her head lolled back. I couldn't stop myself, my lips covered her, my hand delving into her locks of gold. I held her head in place as I plundered her luscious lips.

Her core smells so good, I need to tear these pants off of her, Tet had dropped to his knees and was devouring her cunt through the fabric of her pants. Quickly, he finds the waistband, pulling the pants and undergarment down to the ground. She leans against me, as Tet puts one of her legs over his shoulder, opening her up to him. Through our connection I can feel his utter joy

I come up from kissing her. "And when we have thoroughly fucked you, we will mark you with our teeth." Then I continue with my conquest of her honeyed lips. Our tongues battling for the control yet giving power to each other.

"Will it hurt?" she breathes out when I give her a chance to breathe again.

"I do not think so." I say honestly. Never having had a mate and only a short amount of time to actually research mates and mating with humans. My hands had stolen up her tunic and returned to her bared breasts and I could feel the hardened pebbles of her nipples, as I gently pinch and roll them between my fingers.

I think our mate is nearing her climax. Tet informs me as the mewling and little whines from our mate come louder.

"Oh God! Oh my God! Don't stop… please… please…Don't stop!" She whines as I continue to pinch and pull on her nipples, while I nibble on her neck. She moves her hands to Tet's head, pulling him further into her apex. I can see his movements in his mind as he licks and nibbles on the bud at the top of her cunt, as well as his fingers pushing up into her center curving into that rough spot in her vaginal canal. The more he rubs, the more our mate keens out her pleasure. Until I feel her stiffen in my arms before a final scream, "I…I …OH God! You are my Gods… Oh Lord! Oh Fuck!" and she begins to jerk as she comes completely undone.

As Tet softly licks her clean of her cum: *You will have to try this, Tan. She tastes amazing!*

Before we can start a second round the chime of our door alert goes off. We quickly pull her pants back on. I head to the door. Tet holds our mate up.

We did our job well, he tells me. S*he can barely stand.* Then he moves her to the sitting area. Placing her on his lap. He is relaxed and looks very happy.

"What do you want?" I demand of the crewman holding a tray.

"I was told to bring your first meal here." He looks concerned at me, then to my brother and mate...*I do not like him looking at her.* I tell Tet.

Neither do I, get rid of him I instruct the crew member to put the food on the table and he is across the room quickly. As soon as he puts the tray down, he hesitates. "Sir, the humans were worried about Lady Kelsey."

"Our mate is fine,." Tet is quick to say.

Do you think that wise to announce our mating? I look at him.

If we do not want a mutiny we will explain our actions...your actions. He reminds me of my rash actions.

The ensign gets a look of understanding. "Ah! Congratulations, sirs!"

"You can go now.," I order and he doesn't hesitate to leave.

He was nervous to be in here. I think he can smell the sex, Tet observes.

She is ours...OUR mate. I am emphatic.

I wish they would keep it down. I am so tired here. Tet and I look at each other with surprise. *Our mate hears us!*

"Of course, I hear you" Kelsey says grumpily, "And please keep it down. That was so intense, I just want to sleep a little. OK?"

"We were not talking out loud, my mate." She looks at me with surprise.

"What do you mean, you weren't talking? I could hear you clearly!" She exclaims, with disbelief. Jumping off the lounger.

I look at her and send, my heart, *we weren't talking out loud"*

Chapter Seven – Kelsey

They can talk to me with telepathy! Holy crap! Telepathy and the best orgasm of my life! And they are smiling with definitely smug looks on their face, as they move to box me between them.

"You can hear my thoughts, can't you?" Their smiles widen.

Yes, my heart. Our first connection in our mating. We will know your thoughts and feelings when you are within limited distances, Tan informs me.

"You really don't talk out loud much, do you?" I look at him.

I have Tet, and now you, to verbalize my thoughts. Talking is just loud and inelegant. I communicate better through thoughts. So, yes, you are correct. He gives me a bit of a squeeze from behind.

Tan is a bit of an introvert. Tet adds. My breasts are pressed against his upper abdomen. His chest is at eye level. Feeling like a Kelsey sandwich here…Not a bad feeling, really.

"Well, you don't have to worry about me being an introvert," I say aloud. "I kind of like the sound of my voice. I might have become a singer, if I didn't prefer to study astronomy and astrophysics to musical notation."

Our mate is an astrophysicist? Tan has a big smile on his face. *She is very intelligent to be able to study such complicated field.*

"Well, I have finished my Bachelor's and was working on my Master's generally most jobs need a Doctorate," I sheepishly state.

"I do not know what that means. However, are you interested in star navigation?" Tet asks me.

"That is kind of the dream for many of my classmates." I giggle, "But most of those who can go into space need to join the Military to get a foot in the door with NASA. And I am not really the type the US Military is looking for. Besides, I don't really want to be in the business of warfare."

Most of our military missions are peaceful or peacekeeping. Tan sends to me. *It would give you purpose to work in ship's navigation. Until you have younglings to care for.*

"Excuse me? Younglings?" I am not happy. "You expect *me* to be a brood mare and nanny for a bunch of brats? With all this technology and you have these backwards ideas about women?"

Oh, no, my heart! I just thought you would want to take care of any young we are fortunate to create. Tan begins to back pedal. *I thought...*

"You thought!" I yell, poking him in the chest. "You thought! You thought... I would want to give up work I enjoy to raise babies? Is that what your females do here? Wait for the hubby to come home while going crazy as the brats run around wild, pooping and barfing on everything?"

Or we can hire a nanny? Tet thinks.

"I may want to raise my children!" I am really working myself up. "Just because I don't want to be a brood mare and happy, little housewife, doesn't mean I don't want child…I mean, younglings. I do, but I won't be dictated to." I feel Tan has become more agitated… and aroused… *Hello, is that a banana in your pocket or are you just happy to see me*? I can't help but smirk a bit.

"Female! Make up your mind!" He yells out in that growly voice that makes me so hot.

"When it is time, but as I said, I won't be dictated to." I feel him huffing, his breath hot against the back of my neck. I have a bit of a smile as I think of what he can do to me. But I try not to think too much. If he knows my thoughts he may back off to punish me. True, I am a bit of a brat.

"Yes, you are a brat!' Tet states smirking at me, "Let's eat and we will *discuss* your moving to the quarters of your mates."

"Are you asking or demanding?" I say.

"Female!" Tan yells again. "We are your mates! You need to be with us."

Tet raises his hand. "Tan, remember the claim is her decision. So, by rights, she decides if she will stay in our quarters."

What are you saying? She is our mate; she needs to be with us. Tan is astonished and then a revelation. *I need her here. I need to know that she is safe and in our care, at the very least.* OK, he is being really sweet with that statement, but I am not going to back down just because his cute little vulnerability is melting my insides.

I will be safe, I think. *Am I not on your ship?* I suddenly have an image of what Tan really needs. *Oh, myyyy.* Yeah, I am willing to discuss this whole move in with the new boyfriends thing.

What is this "boyfriends"? Tan asks.

Geez, forgot about the whole telepathy thing. *Is there anyway to turn this off or at the very least, have a bit of privacy in my thoughts?*

Yes, and we will teach you to build a wall of privacy. Tet answers.

"Thank gawds for small favors." I look up at both of them, "Can you two, like, back up a bit? I really would like to go eat a little bit of lunch or whatever meal this is." They immediately back off and lead me to the food on the "dining room" table. I admit to myself that I feel a little bereft without the warmth of their bodies. I sit in one of the big chairs that are built for giants like my aliens…yeah, I guess they are mine…I am not sure about this being tied to these two sticks-in-the-mud for close to 200 years, but I know that I am very attracted to them…and their tongues…yeah, I don't know if it is my pussy controlling this or my brain. However, I have never had a boyfriend that I could share my studies. Even my own parents weren't really enthused by my love of astrophysics. I sometimes think my mom thinks I read astrological signs, not deal in heavy studies of mathematics and physics. So, the delight of these two males at my choice of studies makes me rather pleased that they get it. They sounded proud of my choices. Maybe, I could learn to like this.

The meal is tasty and I am so glad that I am not a picky eater, as I don't recognize any of the dishes on the table. Heck, I don't know how a picky eater would survive in this part of the Universe…Sorry, no pizza or chicken nuggets for you…Just starve you baby

My heart, please move to our quarters, Tet asks.

"What would the ladies think?" I ask. "You know humans don't just shack up with a guy, not the least two guys, they barely know?"

They will be envious that you are mated to the command team of the Patience. Tan tells me. *You know that we will provide you with every comfort.*

"Or they will think I am a slut." I give them a point.

You would be a respected mate. I feel Tan's anguish. *They would not dare call you that name! You are a mate to Akkadianan males. This is how it is done.*

"Listen, I gather that this mating thing is for life, right?" I take a small bite of the green stuff. Kind of like a pudding.

Yes, my heart. They both tell me.

"And your life expectancy is two hundred years." I look at them.

Yes, Kelsey. They reply.

"That is a long time," I say. "I am twenty-one. I am barely legal to drink alcohol on my part of the planet I am from. I have never had a relationship that lasted more than a few months. I don't know if I could handle being in a 150 – 200 year relationship. I flirt and like to party. I don't know anything about being someone you will want to be with for the rest of your lives."

"My heart, you will always be the one we will want," Tet begins. "Now, this flirting? We are not keeping you satisfied if you want to flirt with other males."

I can assure you that you will be well satisfied. Tan gives me a hungry look. *I will taste that sweet cunt every morning and every night. We will fill your womb with young and your heart will sing praises to our cocks.*

"One good orgasm and you think you know how to please me?" I roll my eyes at this.

Shall we show you, my heart? As lovely as that sounds, I begin to think that I may be over my head.

"I like a challenge!" I state. "I will move into your quarters. However, no claiming until I say so. Is this agreed." Tet and Tan nod their agreement and we finish our meal. However, Tan and I just can't help arguing over things. It really turns me on to rile him up. So, I decide to go for the gold, "That's it! I am staying with the ladies and not moving in." Tan jumps up and starts dragging me to the door.

You will move in with us. The decision was made and you will be in our quarters from now on! He starts pulling me to the door as the chime goes off.

Chapter Eight – Tet

I am glad that this part is settled. Our mate will move into our quarters. I just wish she would let us claim her. However, it looks like we will need to do this "courting" thing to win our mate over. She is young and from what other things she has said, I tend to believe that humans do not have fated mates and often leave their mates.

She and Tan are arguing again when the com goes off.

"Captain Bl'Wski... what do you want?" My voice is a bit terse.

"Um, well, sir, I needed to talk to you," It is Commander Max, "I hope I am not disturbing you."

"Not really." As my brother and my mate stomp out of our quarters, I hope they are heading over to get Kelsey's belongings. "Come in, please" I gesture to a chair near the lounger.

"You are sure I am not disturbing you?" He looks worriedly at the couple marching down the hallway and then back to me. I was still distracted by the pair.

"There was nothing left to say at this point." I am resigned to the lack of peace that this mating will mean. "Come and tell me what you are here for?" I lead him into the sitting area and gesture to a chair, before sitting myself.

"Sir, the human, Maryellen, has agreed to be my mate." This is good news. One female will be protected.

"I am glad to hear this." I know I lack enthusiasm, but dealing with my mate has me distracted, "Congratulations, Commander. You have found yourself a mate that will bring you much joy."

"Yes, sir. I hear you have found your mate?" He queries.

I smirk and snort, "Yes, my brother and I have found a mate." I then sigh loudly. "Rin'On, I do not know what we are going to do. This situation is untenable. The female is wild. She causes chaos where ever she goes." I notice the surprise on his face.

"My mate says she is young, so she may still settle down." Rin'On assures me.

"We can't wait for this. If she is our mate we need her to be ready to be a proper mate." I am adamant. "She cannot be flirting with the men, and being disrespectful to her mates. She must obey us without question nor defiance!"

"Um, sir. Humans are not like other females." I look at him.

"Go on." I am intrigued by this information.

"Well, sir, what I have learned from the human females I have worked with in the past and with my own mate: Humans do not like being ordered about." I figured that out. "They will resist strong attempts at authoritarian behavior from males. What we consider discipline. Often they will act like they are acquiescing while they are subverting your authority or worse manipulating you. But they tend to be open or, at least, working for our benefit." I hear the wisdom in his words. "My mate even thinks the criminal funding the Misagians is a female. It seems that, in their history, they had females who drew great power by hiding behind their males and manipulating them from behind the scenes."

"That makes sense, I hadn't thought of that," I respond. "You are truly fortunate to have such a wise mate with the good sense to agree to mating with a worthy male such as yourself." He chuckles.

"Sir, I had to convince her to be my mate. In fact, I had to agree to get reassigned to an on planet duty, after this mission is complete." My shock must have been visible as he nodded. "She was very insistent that she wouldn't allow me to claim her unless I agreed to 'be home every night'. Her first mate, her husband, was a military officer and died while on a mission in a war zone. She didn't want to go through that again."

"I see." Very reasonable.

"Captain…Tet… you need to talk to your mate...woo her," he explains. "You can't just say 'I am your mate and you will do what I say.' I feel that you will find that Kelsey will do everything contrary to your wants and needs until she is courted," Yes…this is true…I will consider this, "and wants to be an asset for you. The more you and Tan bluster, the more she is going to ignore you."

"Why would the gods curse us with such a mate?" I chuckle at this, "Tan isn't going to be happy about this. He really likes order, predictability, and our mate is anything but predictable."

"Well, sir, maybe the gods felt you and your brother need to loosen up a bit." He is on the edge of insubordination, but I think I know where his thought processes are leading, "I find that with

Maryellen, it is important to talk to her, listen to her, and learn how she thinks. It made it easy for me to make decisions that are good for both of us, not just *my* career and *my* life. I have been given the greatest gift. Is it convenient, no. However, she makes me very happy and we haven't actually mated."

"You haven't claimed her yet!" I say, concerned.

"Sir, I told you, I needed to get her to want to be with me." He takes a breath, "Also, I am a father now. We have a youngling to worry about. Which is why I am here. The females will not allow me to sleep in the same room as my mate unless *you* perform a marry ceremony."

"What is a 'marry ceremony'?" I ask.

"It is a Earth custom and they say I can not be with my mate unless I have marry ceremony with her." he explains, "They said that even though we do not have a religious leader on board, there is a precedence for ship's captain to do such a ritual."

"But I do not know how to do this marry ceremony." I am nervous about what this ceremony means.

"Do you think you could ask your mate?" He suggests, "It might be a way to start conversations about humans with her." Yes, this is a good idea. I will ask Kelsey to explain this marry ceremony.

"I will do this." I agree, "When will this ceremony take place?"

"After third shift meal?" He asks, "I really do not want to spend anymore time away from my mate as I am forced to."

"Should we not make a bit more than a simple ceremony?" I suggest, "Maybe a bit of a party will satisfy the females and make them see that the males of the *Patience* will be good mates for them." I smile at the captain's optimism.

"It could not hurt, Sir." He smiles, rises from his seat, and places his hand to his chest before departing my quarters. He has given me a lot to think on. I have already witnessed how Kelsey handles orders. I will need to take time and figure out how to get her to accept her new life.

Tet, where are you two. I need Kelsey.

Be there in a few minutes. I will need to drag her away from her friends.

I heave a big sigh at the thought of what my brother and I will need to do in order to get this human claimed and mated. While I am frustrated, I also have a strange sense of rightness. Like the Universe has a plan for us and it will work out.

Chapter Nine – Kelsey

Tan and I returned to their quarters...I guess, our quarters. Tet is on the lounger with his hand to his brow, as if his thoughts are troubling him. When he looks up and sees us it is like a cloud is lifted from his face.

I am so glad you are here, my heart, he says in my mind.

"How can I help you?" I am just not used to this speaking in the mind thing yet nor having this male look to me for help. They just like ordering me around.

We do not order you around. They both do that think speak thing.

"Yes, yes, you both do," I tell them bluntly. "What is it you need from me? And can you just talk to me out loud?"

"Um, yes, my heart." I do like that endearment. Tet gets a slight smile.

"You really need to teach me how to block you. Now, what is it you need?"

"Commander Max's female…"

"You mean Maryellen?" I correct him.

"Yes. Maryellen." Tet shows a little bit of chagrin at my correction. "She has agreed to be Max's mate. However, the other females say they must have a marry ceremony and …"

"A marriage ceremony!" I squeal, then giggle, "Yeah, Maryellen and the ladies were in the bunk when we got there, so I heard there was to be a wedding."

"Uh…affirmative, my heart," Tet states hesitantly. "and they want me to perform the ceremony"

"That makes sense, since you are the Captain of this ship." I confirm, looking at the confusion in his face, "And you have no clue how to perform this ceremony, do you?"

His head bows bashfully, "No, my heart. I am not too sure about this marry…er, marriage ceremony is done."

"Well, Tet, you are in luck," I say, with a grin, and then I begin with "Yours is the easy part. You just have to stand there looking important and say a few words."

"But what words?" He almost has a whine to his voice.

"OK, here is what I remember from the last wedding I attended. It was my cousin, Brittany's big to-do. Gawds, that was a huge overblown affair. Must of cost Uncle Ralph a bundle." And I start to relay the description of the wedding ceremony. Omitting the stupid parts. Maybe, adding a few things that were better. As we talked about the marriage ceremony, Tet wrote notes on his com pad. It confuses them that we had a ceremony for mating. I guess when you have mating marks things are a bit different for your

My heart, will you need such a ceremony when we claim you? Tan relays to me.

"OH, HELL NO!" I almost yell. "If… and that is a big if… I let you claim me, I really do not need all that big show of wealth and 'look at me, I'm a bride' in a big white dress. Nope, if your culture just fucks and bites, well, that will be good enough for me. I just think I will be happy that you want me for me."

It seemed like both males were relieved that I wasn't into the whole wedding thing. Besides, I am still not sure if I am ready for the til death do we part business… literally, until we die we are bound to each other…Wow…just wow. That is just a lot to take in. I didn't know too many people who remained together for more than ten years. Definitely not my parents. Dad was on his third wife and Mom just said, "I take care of my children. I don't need a man." Which was true. She worked 16-20 hour days as a lawyer and made the bucks, but was she happy? I know that her parents were. Mee-maw and Pawpaw were together until their deaths a few years ago in a car accident. The few times Mom let me go to her family's farm to visit, they were so affectionate. But Mom would dismiss it as, "That is just their generation. Your grandmother would be so much happier if she had finished her degree instead of getting married and having kids." I was never really sure. Mee-maw always looked happy and she took joy in my mom and her siblings. However, she and Mom went at it because Mom chose a career over family. I don't know. Dad was busy with his girlfriends and neglected us, so maybe, Mom just wanted to make sure that we were protected. Unlike his mother, who committed suicide when my paternal grandfather took off with a hairdresser he impregnated leaving her destitute and thinking it was all her fault. Mom was protecting herself.

What kind of dishonorable male deserts his mate? Oops, forgot about that tapping into my thoughts thing.

"It was years ago, but you can see why I am not sure about this whole mates for life thing. Humans haven't had really good luck in that." I tell my mates…yeah, I am getting used to the idea. "Now, teach me how to block you."

"It is fairly easy…" And he begins explaining the way to keep my thoughts private.

Chapter Ten – Tan

That was a lovely wedding," my mate stated as we walked into our room.

They denuded the garden of all it's blossoms! I am not amused by the vandalism of our carefully manicured green space.

"Relax, they will bloom again and the Officer's Mess looked beautiful." She looks down on the dress she is wearing. "Even this bridesmaid dress ain't too bad. My dress for Brittany's wedding was the worst. No one was going to outshine her in those puke green sacks."

You look stunning and much prettier than the…bride. Tet tells her. Kelsey places her hand on his chest.

"You just won yourself some points for flattery, my boy…er…male." I note that she is a little more pliable than usual.

My heart, have you been imbibing in alcohol. She giggles.

"Only a little bubbly!" She replies.

What is bubbly? I have a feeling I know but I need her to confirm.

"I don't know what you call it, but it reminds me of champagne, only green instead of gold."

You are drunk on Mitirian Wine, my heart. I shake my head with a bit of a smile. Tet has a bit of a rueful smile too. *I do not know this champagne, but I do know that someone as small as you should not drink more than a small glass of Mitirian Wine.*

"I think you two are so yummy!" Kelsey points her finger between us, "I am not small." She is emphatic, then pats her behind. "I have cushion for pussshin'. I am big enough to take you two on." Shakely she puts her finger over her mouth. "Shhhh. Don't tell anyone, this is a secret…Even though you two have serious sticks up your ass, I think I am falling in wuv…love wit…with you. I shouldn't…You are way too bossy…" My heart is beating quickly, she loves us.

My heart, Tet starts, *let's get you to bed*

"Hmmmm, bed…" she mumbles. "I will give both of you amazing blowjobs…because you need a reward for those orgasms you gave me…Or maybe, we can fuck all night." Stars! My cock hardens at her drunken mumbling, but this can not happen, not while she is drunk. I swing her off her feet and stalking toward the bedroom.

"Hey!" She says. "Maryellen is the bride, why you carrying mee over the threshold."

I do not know what you are talking about, but I do not want you to stumble and fall, I respond.

"OK, but I am too heavy for you to carry." Her eyes are heavy lidded. She is falling asleep. As I get to the bed, I gently stand her up and start to undress her. Tet comes into the room carrying a glass of water.

My heart, drink this please. She, dutifully, follows Tet's instructions, drinking the whole glass then sits on the bed where I had drawn back the covers. I lift her up and place her in the middle of the large bed. She immediately falls asleep and I turn to Tet.

She loves us.

Of course, she does, she is our mate. We just need to figure out how to get her to submit to us. I look at him.

I do not think it is going to be easy. We need to get her to want to submit to us. Then an odd thought hits me, *Or maybe, we need to submit to her?*

Can we even consider such a thing?

I do not know, but I know she is ours and we are hers. I think it will bear considering.

Chapter Eleven – Kelsey

I wake up with a light headache, almost a hangover. My eyes were not quite ready to open but I remember drinking some water, so that is good. I remember, Tan carrying me into the room and I was talking to both of my males. I don't remember what I said. Although, I know that I am a really chatty drunk.

Then I notice that I am warm on both sides. That is when I try opening my eyes, I notice that there is soft lighting. That is a blessing for my poor eyes. Suddenly, I notice two weights on me: one on my waist and one over my chest.

Um…where are my clothes? I think.

We removed them for your comfort, my heart. Tet gives me a sleepy thought.

That is when the weight on my chest shifts and I notice the heat on my back includes a very hard presence making itself known against my bare ass. I will admit that I am tempted to wiggle against that large morning wood. The hand on my waist gives me a soft squeeze.

"Did we…" Trying to ask if we had sex.

No, my heart, you were drunk. You could not consent. This time it is a sleepy Tan that answers. The heat source to my front snuggles closer to me, showing that I now have a woody to the front of me and one behind me. Somehow, I know this will be my life and I am not complaining. In fact, I choose to have a little fun.

I wiggle my body so I am on my back. Then I slip my hands to both of those large cocks, grasping each in my hands. I am impressed that I am not able to completely close my hands around these girthy shafts, but I am still able to begin sliding my hands up and down those turgid lengths. Tet and Tan move in tandem as they move closer to me and begin to message my breasts.

You know where this will lead, my heart? Tan asks.

"To your pleasure?" I ask faking naivety. Tet moves his hand from my breast, down my body, to the apex of my thighs.

Your pleasure, too. But if we keep this up we will fill you with our cocks. Tet informs me.

"No claiming, right?" I love the idea of fucking them both but I am still not on board with the lifetime commitment.

No, no claiming. We can control ourselves until you let us claim you. Tan starts to push his hips into my hand, upping the friction.

"Can you really?" I challenge, as I let go just enough to get on my knees and I bend over Tan's staff while I am still working Tet's cock. I lick the precum that pearls on Tan's tip. Slowly, I lick the head of his penis then I take it into my mouth and begin to suck. I smile as I hear t he catch in Tan's breathing. His eyes are open and he is watching my movements, as I pleasure him.

You are a miracle, my heart, that feels so good.

Tet removes my hand from his cock and swiftly shifts my hips to face him, as he licks my slit, I moan from sheer pleasure. My mouth is full of Tan and when I moan, he feels it.

I continue to take more of Tan, while Tet sucks and nibbles at my clit. His fingers begin to stroke into my core. One then two fingers fill my vagina, stretching, scissoring and pressing on my g-spot. It doesn't take long before my orgasm is building.

I begin to play with Tan's balls as I hum over his cock. I hear his pleasure and feel his need building as I lick and suck, taking him into my throat working to relax my gag reflex, so I take all his length and he is long…and wide.

*My heart, my heart…I am…*Cum shoots out of his cock as I swallow it all down until I can't take anymore, because I am screaming as my own orgasm hits. Tet licking up all my cream, then he moves to put his girth at my entrance.

Do you want my cock, my heart? Tet communicates with me, *Tell me you want my cock inside you.*

"Yes, take me now, Tet!" And with that he pushes his full length into my cunt. "Oh gods, yes…yes," I scream as he pounds into me. I know that I may regret the roughness of his passion but it feels so good.

Tan, our mate's cunt is so tight… she takes me so well. I feel pride at his thoughts as his cock hits my cunt so right I am keening in joy of this primal sensation.

Tan moves into position to rub my breasts and rolling my nipples through his fingers. Tet withdraws and before I can complain, he flips me over taking my ankles and putting them over his shoulders, as he pushes back into me.

Tan takes advantage of my new position, he straddles my belly. Pushing my large breasts together over his quickly recovered cock. As he fucks my tits, he bends down and gives me a kiss. My hands reach his head as I weave my fingers into his short hair, just enough to grasp. Our tongues tangle, as he continues to use my large breasts for his pleasure.

Tet has become frantic in his movements; my orgasm is close. As if sensing this, Tet reaches between us and begins circling and pinching my clit. Tan swallows my scream as my climax overtakes my body. My channel tightens, squeezing Tet's cock. Feeling the warmth of his seed painting my uterus causes me to orgasm again.

When Tet is emptied he withdraws and Tan replaces him. They may be twins, but they fill me differently…wonderfully, but different… Tan's girth stretches me ever farther than his heavily endowed brother. I don't know how I can take both of them when the time comes for the claiming. However, that is a momentary thought as he slowly slides in and out of me. The slowness is tantalizing and frustrating, as he keeps that pace that builds me up, but not taking me over the edge into another. He has spread my legs so wide and wrapped them around his hips. I broadcast my need by trying to pull him in with my heels. He gives my butt a sharp slap.

No, my heart, I have waited too long for this. I intend to savor your tight cunt. Tan's smile is too beautiful as he continues that maddening pace.

Tet has moved to my side and bends down to kiss me...Damn these guys know how to kiss. He dominates the kiss until I am breathless. Panting and moaning from both of these males overwhelming with their complete take over of my body. My orgasm is building again as I feel Tan's rhythm increasing. My hand reaches for Tet's cock as his tongue plunders my mouth. Both of them are doing amazing things to my body. I want to reciprocate, but Tan keeps his rhythm just at that point that keeps me needy and Tet has his hips just out of reach as his tongue dominates my mouth and his hands take control of my breasts...

"Oh gods, yes! Yes!" I scream into Tet's mouth then he is nibbling down my neck and over my chest until he sucks one nipple into his mouth.

It is like electricity shoots from my breast to my clit. I am moaning and keening. I must have tightened my channel, as Tan loses control and starts pumping harder and faster. Tet sucks at the other nipple and his hand reaches down to my clit. He and Tan work me up until I am screaming both their names. Tan roars as he comes shooting streams of cum into my core, my channel tightening, and I climax again.

I am spent. I hope we don't have much to do this morning. Because that was… I think I am dead and in heaven…

Chapter Twelve – Tet

I lay with my mate between my brother and I. All of us sated by our activities this morning. Using the block on Kelsey, I speak to my brother.

I do not care what we have to do but we must claim our mate, I tell him.

You keep telling me, she has the choice. Do we dare claim her without that permission? Tan is just dumbfounded by this miracle of our mate as I am.

No, we can't force her. However, we need to make sure she sees the logic of letting us bond her to us. I am sure we will find the way convince her.

We should probably rise and check in with the third Shift. Tan is being practical. All I want to do is drive my cock back into our mate while my teeth and venom penetrate that perfect neck.

We will get there soon, Brother. Tan has a grin on his face, as he gets up and heads to the sanitary room and begins our day.

"My heart, it is time to wake." I lightly shake Kelsey.

"No…Not awake." I smile at her mumbling.

"Come, my heart, we must start the day." Pulling back the covers, I find myself wrestling with my mate for the covers she is snuggled in. I am astonished by her fierce determination to stay asleep. Tan comes back in as I am still trying to wrest the covers from our mate.

Here, I will grab the covers, you grab our mate. Tan states his idea.

I grab our mate as Tan snakes the covers. There is a bit of a moan then a scream.

"What the fuck are you doing?!" Kelsey screams, as I carry her to the sanitary room, then deposit her in the shower, turning it on full blast. "You assholes! I was sleeping!"

"Yes, my heart, but now, it is time to start our day." Grabbing the cleansers, I start rubbing it into her hair and skin, before cleaning myself. I rinse her off and then myself, before turning off the shower and walking through the dryer unit. When we are clean, I carry her back into our room and throw some clothes at her to dress as I pull on my uniform. She doesn't speak; just looks daggers at us.

I guess she isn't a morning person after all, huh? Tan relays with a smirk.

"Ya think? I was warm and snug …and…and you two woke me!" My mate is really in a twist.

We needed you to come with us to the Officer's Mess, I let her know. *We will let you spend the day with your friends as we see to our duties.*

"Oh really, I am to play bridge with the girls while my strong males go to work?" I am confused.

"No, my heart, you won't be on the bridge with us," I correct her. "You will stay with the other females. You will be less likely to stay out of trouble there."

She sneers. "First off, bridge is a game that bored housewives used to play. Secondly, why can't I start working for navigation. Thirdly, I am not going to be your plaything that you put in a box when I am not useful."

Tan is ready to burst. "You, human, are going to do as we say. Tet and I need to make sure you are safe! And do not say you are the play thing, like you weren't there right with us!"

"Oh, so now, you are slut shaming me for enjoying sex with you two!" She yells.

"NO! You were magnificent! You are not a slut…whatever that is. You are our mate. We must protect you until we have claimed you. And even then we will always protect you." Tan stomps to the door. "Come, mate! You, my heart, will eat your first shift meal with us, then spend time with the other humans."

"You can't order me around! I am only going with you because I need some food, now that I am awake. Thanks to you!".

And with that, our amazing morning turns into another argument. I can only hope the day gets better as I follow behind the angry pair.

Chapter Thirteen – Ab'Nel

My Commanding Officer is an idiot… and he smells unnatural. Rumor has it he is under the powers of witch. Must be under a spell of some type, because before his meeting with our benefactors I caught him in a bathhouse using the baths. Misagian cruisers do not have cleansing units. We do not use them. That is something our females do. We are males and baths take our virility from us. At least that is what our priests say. Never having fucked anything, let alone a female, I do not know.

Our Captain came back from his meeting smelling from that unnatural smell and smiling triumphantly. I do not know who he meets with and I do not trust that smile. Did his contacts give him a female? I know he was hoping to get a mate when he gets back from this mission. But what if he is being paid in female flesh and we are not getting paid at all? Well, I better see a paycheck soon or I will kill him and take over. I am through with our leadership getting perks and we, the ones doing the work, are getting nothing of value.

"Ab'Nel, my friend!" Captain Schnel'Dn says. "I have great news. When we get the cargo back from the Galactic Council Station, I will be in a great situation! And you will benefit as my second-in-command, my boy."

"I am glad to know this," I state cautiously.

"You should be. However, we need to be prepared." He begins to tell me his plans to sneak onboard the station and hide in a safehouse, provided by friends of the Councilmember from Misagia. I am to stay on the ship and make sure that our cloaking tech is working. "Our benefactors paid a pretty penny for it and we don't want the wrong people getting a hold of it, now do we."

"No, Sir." I really can't bear the smell of him at this point. I will report him to our councilmember if things go wrong. The thought makes me smile.

"Now, my boy." I hate when he calls me that. I am two spans younger than him, not thirty. "If something goes wrong, I need you to do something for me."

"I would be honored to, Sir." I lied. I will enjoy doing things to dishonor this male.

"If something should, in the unlikely chance, there are two things I need of you. Wait a moment. Come with me." He takes me aside and into his private space off the deck, Closing the door "The first is to pack up my room and send it to my brother, Co'Gn. He will know what to do with things and don't mention anything you find. Understand?"

I nod, though depending on the information I find, I am not above a little blackmail.

"Next, there is a memory chip in my office, behind that panel." He points to the left and I see a small maintenance panel. "It is important that you, as Captain, take that chip and use it wisely, as I know only you can. My boy, you are not like the others, and if you follow my instructions, you will be rich and powerful."

"Sir?" I am intrigued. He laughs.

"No, No, my boy...Don't get any ideas." He tugs me under his arm and looks around the room like someone else is there. "If I am successful, you will be Captain and will be given the chip. Just don't blow it, by being too curious at this point. Patience is the key! Now, go get us heading to the Council Station. Remember, use the cloaking drive."

"Yes, Sir." I am curious, but I can wait. Things may workout in my favor if I just bide my time.

Chapter Fourteen – Kelsey

I follow my boyfriends…mates…husbands… I don't know what to call them, but they are mine…into the Officer's Mess. The other ladies are all there, except for Maryellen…That's a surprise…She gets to sleep in but I don't, lucky bitch.

Now, my heart, you know that they are in a mating frenzy currently, Tan explains to me.

We might not see them for a week. Tet adds.

"You two shouldn't be reading my mind." I complain. "but that is one hell of a booty call."

"Hey, Kelsey, what booty call are you talking about?" Cara signals to me, "I mean, you look like you got some." She smiled like a cat with cream. My cheeks begin to heat up.

Are you alright, my heart, Tan asks, *Your cheeks are turning red.*

Shush you! I think.

"Cara, I am sure the ladies aren't interested in my love life," I demure.

"Oh no, *querida*, we want all the deets," Yaretzi says with enthusiasm.

"Well, then, you better get your own Akkadianans!" I give my friends a stern look. They just laugh and giggle and look at my me and my men with good humor.

"You did say you were going to have two males. Didn't you?" Victoria didn't sound amused. "it just isn't right. One man and one woman. That is God's plan."

"Female, you forget where you are." Tan is upset.

"Tan, please forgive Victoria. Like I told you situations, like ours are still unusual on Earth." I give Victoria a look and she has the good sense to look down.

"As long as I don't have to live in sin with two men, I guess it is okay." Victoria mumbles, "It truly is up to God to judge."

"Yes, Victoria," I agree. "I seem to remember that that is what the Bible says."

Tet, Tan, and I move to the other side of the ladies and sit down. There are a few crew members in the mess and one of the Mess Officer's bring us our meal. I give him a slight smile in gratitude. "Thanks, Ar'Ti!" The male just nodded quickly, shifting his eyes to both of the males I sit between then ran off, back to the Kitchen.

"I wonder what up with Ar'Ti?" I say. "He was so friendly the past few days."

"He knows his place and your place in our lives," Tet tells me.

"You mean, he can't even say 'hi' to me?" I ask.

Tet sniffs and states, "It is not appropriate for him to associate with the Command Team's mate."

"That is so fucked up!" I yell. "I need *friends*."

And you have friends, a kitchen scut isn't an appropriate friend, Tan replies, *The humans are currently the best friends for you.*

"You are a snob, Tan." I tell him.

I don't know what that is and I don't care. He just looks at me. *It is the way of things on board a well run ship. You will get used to it.*

"And you wonder why I get so pissed off with you," I hiss.

"My heart, can we eat in peace?" Tet asks.

"I don't know, can you get chuckles over here to not remind me what an asshole he is?" The ladies gasp at that statement.

"Um, Kelsey... You might want to be a bit nicer to the commander," Millie says quietly.

"Yeah, You are starting to sound like a bitch," says Yaretzi. "The poor guy isn't saying a word and your calling him an asshole."

"You have no idea what is going on or you would go ballistic on this male." Tan has a bit of a smirk on his face. He has the good sense to huff when I elbow him.

We are finish up our meal when Tet and Tan get up, each giving me a quick kiss and head out to the bridge. Yaretzi swiftly moves in on me, as the other crewmembers follow their command team out of the Officer's Mess.

"Gurrll, now that they have left, you have to tell me what is going on," she says. "Inquiring minds really need to know."

I look over and see Jaycee, Maryellen's four-year-old. Nope, not gonna be that gal that spills the beans and definitely in front of a child. So, I just smile.

"They didn't beat you or force anything on you did they?" I laughed at Yaretzi.

"No, no, none of that. It was all consensual and it was good. However, there are some side affects that showed up without them claiming me." I tried to stay as vague as possible.

"Side effects?" She asks.

"I have a telepathic link to Tet and Tan," I tell her.

"So, *that* is why you were calling Tan an asshole." She asks, "He is saying something to upset you and we can't hear it? Wow, that is fucked up."

"And Tan hates to talk, so he deliberately speaks in my mind." I smile about what a jerk he is.

"So, um, two of them, huh?" This time it is Cara in her soft southern drawl. I sigh, nod my head, and give a "A…yeee…pp."

"Then we really can't talk in front of the c-h-i-l-d." She says with a wink.

"Definitely not, and I will just say all will be good, if I could just get those sticks out of their as…Butts." I give her a knowing look, "If you know what I mean."

Yaretzi giggles. "That good, huh."

"Better," my grin went from sly to shit eating, as I remember my night with my males… yep, definitely mine.

Just then, the door to the Mess opens, allowing Maryellen and Rin'On to enter. As one, all our jaws drop as we see Maryellen's skin…it is red…not blushing red…nope, that is some serious strawberry red!

"Girl! What did he do to you!" Michelle exclaimed as she rushed to Maryellen's side, just as Jaycee runs up also.

"Mommy! You're red!" She exclaims. "Just like my new daddy." Maryellen was indeed bright red and looked a lot like her husband…I mean, mate.

"Yes, I am, my bug," Maryellen affirms. "It seems that when a marriage is successful…Well, the mommy turns the same color as the daddy." She looks at all of us ladies. "Something to think about ladies."

"My lad…Maryellen," Lt. Commander B'Jox begins, "Only Caeterin and Ir'Invins change colors when…" …*That is good to know*… He looks at the newlyweds, then nervously at the four-year-old human, "…well… um…when the mating… is real…"… Y*eah, watch what you say around that kid, she is a smart one*…

"Mommy, what is mating?" …D*idn't I say she is a smart one?* …

"Mating is what they call marriage here." …*Good catch, Mom!*...

"So, when I get married, I will turn a cool color?" I just sit back and watch the show…Too bad we don't have popcorn.

"I don't know, baby. It seems that Rin'On's species is one that is special," she starts, then she squats to Jaycees level and whispers into her ear. The widening of the kid's eyes and the opening of her mouth tells me something is up. The kid starts jumping up and down.

"Mommy and Daddy…can I tell everyone?" She shakes with expectation, "*Please.*"

Maryellen has a twinkle in her eye, "I think you can make the announcement."

"Announcement?" Several of the ladies call.

"I am going to be a big sister!!!" Jaycee squeals in a voice that has several of crew holding their hands over their ears. …*OMG, Maryellen is preggers?* …I suddenly feel a smugness coming from Tet and Tan…

This is good news. Rin'On's mate shall be undoubtably safe,. Tet states.

I can't wait until it is our turn, Tan adds.

Well, don't get any big ideas. I don't even know if I want to get pregnant…ever! I feel Tan's ire rise at that thought and it makes me just a tad satisfied. Blocking him, before I allow my real feelings on having children come through.

"He already knocked you up?" Yaretzi and I say in tandem.

"Yes, it seems I am pregnant," Maryellen says. "I don't even have to take a test in six weeks, because…" She gestures to her face and body. "Seems this is the Caeterin pregnancy test. It happens immediately. Or close enough, I woke up looking like this."

"Will you look like this forever?" Michelle asks. "I will need to give you a check up as soon as I can get into the med bay.

The Chief Medic is a bit territorial from what I hear." They begin to talk Obstetrics.

"She just got knocked up." Yaretzi complains as Michelle leads Maryellen to a table. We all just follow behind. "She has nine to ten months to eat and rest. I want to know what that guy did to you. Spill the beans."

"Well, first off. It may not be a full nine month pregnancy." Maryellen reveals. "Rin'On says that Caeterin pregnancies last only six months."

"Really?" Cara pipes up. "Well, ain't that a bit of a humdinger. I know my mama would have liked to have short pregnancies. Cissy nearly drove her crazy in her eighth month with her kicking and moving. Mama told the doc to tie her tubes so tight nothing got through for the last eight years. Daddy appreciated that because five kids was enough he said."

"My *papá* would not ever be satisfied with so few babies." Victoria stated a discussion of whose mom had what kind of pregnancy broke out. It was looking like it could get heated between Victoria and Yaretzi, when Maryellen shut it down…tactfully, I might add. That woman is perfect. I hope Tet and Tan don't expect me to be perfect like Maryellen. That is just too high a bar.

"Well, I just hope that this pregnancy is only six months. Jaycee cooked for nine and a half, so I think six sounds heavenly." Maryellen says.

"Now, I really want to give you a check up," Michelle says. "If you can pop in six months *and* the father is so big, this baby will grow quickly. We will want to monitor you for most of the pregnancy. It will help in future pregnancies. Especially, if you two chose to have more children... I mean, younglings...that is."

"Let's get through this one first. Six months is a long ways away and we don't know where we will be then," Maryellen states with a chuckle. I wonder if I could have children with Tet and Tan. Would they all be twins?

No, my heart, only males come as twins. Females are always singles. Tan lets me know smugly that he heard my thoughts. *However, I am glad that you are thinking of the possibility. I look forward to fucking you while you are large with our younglings.*

Shit, that sounds amazing, then I start blushing as I remember where I am as squeeze my thighs together. *You need to quit listening in, it is rude*, I tell him. I feel his humor.

My heart, I can only hear you and you broadcast so loud. That is when I block him again.

We continue to eat and chat. There is good natured teasing of the newly married Maryellen. As much as can happen with a four-year-old in the room. Then Victoria gets her nose in a twist and makes a stupid comment that gets Yaretzi riled. Seriously, I like Victoria, but she is going to have to lighten up with all that Catholic guilt crap. We aren't on Earth and the only mating material don't have a clue about Judeo-Christian tradition. Then Maryellen shuts it down...Told you, she is perfect...

"Ladies, we are all going to have to find a way to live and live well in this new circumstances. None of us are where we planned to be this time last year. I mean, I don't think any of us had a clue this could happen…"

"I could," a soft voice at the end of the table almost whispered. All of our heads snap around as we realize that Millie just spoke. Half the time I forget Millie is there because she is so quiet.

"You could, Millie?" Maryellen asks. "How could you have imagined this?" She gave a shy smile and shrugged a bit.

"Because I read alien and monster romance books." We lean forward to listen because her voice is almost too soft. "Also, I used to write them, until the fantasy of being abducted became a bit too real."

"Good for you, girl!" I exclaim. "Were they full of weird peens and spicy sex?"

"Ixnay on the exsay, Kels." Yaretzi nods to Jaycee. Luckily, the kid is playing with her toys, not seeming to pay attention to boring adult talk.

"Oh sorry!" I say with a bit of a wince. "I forgot she was there."

"It's OK. She isn't paying attention to us." Maryellen then asked Millie, "So, what got you into reading and writing these kind of books?"

Millie begins to tell the story of what got her into writing. Thanks to a friendly librarian, she was able to escape from a bad marriage and had enough money to live off of while she rebuilt her life…Then, like the rest of us her stories of alien abductions became real.

Millie is telling her story to a rapt audience, when suddenly we hear an explosion then feel the shaking of the ship. An alarm then sounds and we are all wide eyed when Maryellen comes through again. "Ladies! Remain calm and wait for instructions."

"Approaching GFC Station 5, please stay at your stations until connection, unless in section 2…Section 2 evacuate to Section 4 Officer's Mess and secure our guests for landing…"

Within a few moments, several crew members enter the mess and gesture for us to come to the walls where seats pop out, and we are strapped in. Not all the crew members are walking properly, a few look a bit worse for wear. They stumble to the other wall or are helped to the wall where they are strapped in. All the women look at those injured crew members helplessly.

"What happened?" I hear Maryellen ask, as we are all being strapped into the jump seats along the wall

"Explosion in section 2, my lady," The crewmember quietly states.

"There are injured here. What can we do to help?" Maryellen asks, always thinking of others. Maybe, when I grow up, I can be like her.

"There are dead and those injured far worse than these males, my lady," He states. "There are medics getting the living to medical. They will tend these when we have landed. You just need to stay here. We don't need you females getting hurt as we get this old lady into the spaceport. It is going to be a bit bumpy." With that the ship begins to shake and roll. I am glad we are strapped in. Bumpy is definitely an understatement, as the movement tosses us around like laundry in the dryer. Without the straps, we would hit the ceiling, then the floor, then the ceiling again, I am pretty sure. While a few of the women looked a little green around the gills, we all appear to be ok.

My heart, are you alright? Tan and Tet ask together.

Well, I didn't barf, but that landing could have been a little smoother, I respond.

Chapter Fifteen – Tet

Tan and I strode onto the Bridge. Our top officers had finished their change over procedures with the previous shift and were monitoring any anomalies reported.

Navigation, report!" I call out once I am seated in the command chair.

"Sir, we are within less than a quarter solar from the Galactic Federation Council's Space Station," Lt. Oh' Nek, bridge navigation, states.

That is a relief. Tan stands behind me.

"Engineering, report!" I just want to get this part of our day over with. Reports give me an idea of how the ship is running and where I need to crack skulls together.

"Sir, all systems appear to running correctly, but there is an abnormality in life support systems," my bridge officer reports. "Chief Hr'Rcki is looking into the anomaly, but has not classified it as yet. He says he will let you know when he knows, Sir."

Typical chief engineer, no respect for the officers, but he loves this ship as much as I do, so I don't get too upset with his insolence. As we continue the reports, I can feel our mate with her friends discussing the pregnancy of Commander Max's mate.

That was quick, Tan notes with a grin. *I hope we are as lucky...or not.*

I look back at him with a grin. Tan has a little back and forth with our mate. We can tell she is not opposed to breeding with us, but I also sense her need to lead us on a merry chase before she is willing to settle done. I block her as I tell my brother, *Don't worry, we will tame our wild human.*

You better hope it is before she has us tamed. I look at him in horror at the thought. Would we ever get used to her whirlwind nature?

Probably not, says my brother.

Suddenly, several relay alarms go off right before an explosion causes the ship to shake.

"Engineering!" I call. "What is going on."

"Sir, there was an explosion in Section 2." The ensign at the engineering station calls back, "There are several injuries and two deaths, reported at this time."

"Put me through to Chief Engineer Hr'Rcki!" I order.

"Yes, Sir,"says the Ensign.

"Captain," Hr'Rcki responds to the hail, "I really do not have time for this social call...Sir."

"I understand that Chief!" I reply. "Do we need to evacuate?"

"No, Sir, the old girl is flying still and will make it to the Council Station," He assures me. "It will be a rough landing, but have everyone strap in and we will make it."

"Thank you, Chief. I expect a report when we land." I thank him before shutting down the comm. I feel my mate's fear, but she is fine for the moment. I have 350 crew members to worry about currently. Tan sends out the order for all personnel to strap in, as I prepare the bridge for landing procedures. Including letting the Council Station know that we are coming in hot due to an unexpected event. The timing of this explosion is too convenient to be a coincidence.

The Chief didn't lie when he said the landing would be rough. It was more than rough. Tan and I checked on Kelsey together, my heart, *are you alright?*

Well, I didn't barf, but that landing could have been a little smoother. I don't know what she means by "barf", but it sounds unpleasant, so I assume she is alright.

It takes several units to get reports from all stations. The human females were all in the mess at the time of the explosion and all were strapped down for landing. It seems only section two was affected by the explosion, but Tan and I along with Commander Max were requested to section two by Chief Engineer Hr'Rcki.

As we strode down the corridors to the lifts, Tan and I take a moment to make sure our mate stayed safe.

Chapter Sixteen - Kelsey

We *think it would be advisable if you stay with the ladies in the Officer's Mess. We will be busy here.* Tet and Van speak with one voice in my head. So freaky.

I will discuss this with Maryellen. She will probably agree. However, Michelle left with the big purple dude already, I respond.

Commander O'Jectic took the female medic to the Medical wing? Tet said. I could feel his surprise. *He was quite adamant that humans didn't belong in his medical bay.*

Yeah, well, given the good work that Michelle did here, I don't think that is an issue. I will let Maryellen know your wishes.

I walk to Maryellen and say, "Captain and Commander Bl'Wski suggest we stay here for the time being. They are doing sweeps of the ship and getting a feel for what is needed."

"How did they contact you?" Her brows rise in surprise.

"They can talk to me in my brain," I admit.

"What? Telepathy? They have a telepathic link to you? Did they claim you?" She whispers to me.

"Not yet, but they say I am their mate and well, along with the marks, we have done enough to start a bond. So, yeah, telepathy." I am so uncomfortable having to tell her about my almost mating.

"Are they abusive?" She asks with concern for me. "Did they rape you?"

"Oh, no. It was mostly consensual. They are just bossy...They both are so bossy," I confess. "I am 21 years old. I like flirting and partying. Both of them have sticks up their asses and it is really frustrating."

She gives me that perfect mom look and tells me, "Well, they are the commanding officers of this ship. That is a lot of responsibility."

"Yeah, I know and I understand that part. But they act like I need to be a good little robot and march lock step with them. They are stifling me, while they are doing... Well, I won't go there." I remember that there is a child nearby.

"I appreciate that." She nods sympathetically then asks. "So do you like them?"

"I want to say 'no', but to be honest, they turn me on like none of my human boyfriends," I have blocked them, but I am nervous about saying this out loud, so I whisper, "I think I have always needed two dominant males." I wink at her, then return to sit with the ladies. And that is when we hear the call to evacuate the ship. Finally, a way off this bucket.

Chapter Seventeen – Kelsey

My com goes off and with a clipped "Yes?" I answer. It is Commander Max.

"Captain, the chief engineer says the ship needs to be evacuated immediately." The Chief Engineer begins explaining what is happening in the environmental compartments. I am becoming more and more suspicious of this "anomaly".

It does seem very convenient, Tan agrees with me.

"Do we know what caused this?" I ask the Chief.

"Not until we get in there," Says Chief Hr'Rcki. "That's why we need the ship evacuated. The gas will start destroying the life support systems and nothing will stop it."

Fuck, that means securing the humans, Tan is concerned. *There is no way this is a coincidence.*

"Fine, I will make the evacuation call in five units. Will that be acceptable Chief Hr'Rcki?"

"Yes, Sir." The Gurtanian chief answers in the affirmative.

Back on a private com with the Marine Commander, "Max, do you have a schematic of the Council station?"

"Yes, Sir." He sends it to me via the com.

"Can you find a safe space for the females? So we don't have them wandering the Council Station."

"Yes, Sir. There is a large storage space to the right of the ship." I look at the indicated space on the schematic.

"Perfect. Have the females escorted there by the ship's security. We can join them when we have finished shutting down non-essential systems." He has security before we cut the link.

I quickly call into the Station command team and let them know the plan then make the announcement on the ship wide com, "Prepare to evacuate the ship. All assigned engineers will report to Chief Hr'Rcki for hazard suits and duty stations." Looking at the schematic before me I begin to designate locations. "Medical personnel escort all injured personnel to the third Section medical facility in the Council Center. Officer's Mess please wait for the ship's security detail to escort you to a safe space on the space station. Non-assigned crew, all exits are open, please exit in an orderly fashion and gather in the fourth section crew quarters. This is an order for the safety of all. Any non-authorized personnel will be imprisoned at a Galactic Federation penitentiary after court martial. Thank you for complying." Like I give them any choice.

Commander Max meets us as we are striding through the corridors. Just as we are leaving the ship our coms go off simultaneously.

"What?" I am the first to answer.

"Captain, I have just sent you what we found, when we started removing panels."

"That was really fast," Commander Max notes.

"Well, I was monitoring the evacuation and we started as soon as you were the last on board." Typical Chief we are still on board and he isn't waiting for the command officers safety.

"Is that a bomb?", Max asks.

"Well, what is left of one." The chief confirms, "It had enough of a charge to destroy a localized area, without taking out the whole ship. Someone wanted us grounded."

I knew it! Tan feels triumphant then concerned.

Just what we were thinking. Definitely an inside job.

Suddenly, we hear a blast from the store room door. Commander Max starts running and growing as we hear the shouts of his mate and youngling. His beast is let loose and we just follow behind. Hoping our mate is safe. Finding the Misagian Pirates in the room, we quickly dispatch them all... Well, Max in his beast form tears most of them apart. We are just there for a bit of clean up. We try to see if we can get answers, but if there are any left they escaped.

"Where's our mate?" I ask Maryellen.

"Kelsey?" She says. "I don't know, she, Millie and Yaretzi were in the back looking at the wall, there is a hidden passage, I think they snuck out. Hey, can't you just use your telepathy to ask her where she is?"

Kelsey, where are you? I am not happy with her response.

Scram! You buzzkill. I don't want to talk to either of you! I am surprised.

"No," I let Maryellen know, then I lean in close and whisper. "She just keeps telling us to 'scram' and that Tan and I are 'buzzkills'. What does that even mean?" I can tell that Max's mate is trying to hide her amusement at our predicament.

"I think she was feeling a little stifled and, maybe thought it would be better to go off with the girls. Remember she is still young. An adult, but still a young one."

"Frustrating." I sigh heavily, "I need to contact the Senior Council and advise him of the situation." I move off to the other side of the room and make the call.

"Senior Councilor. I am sorry I don't have a lot of time. We have three missing humans," I advise Councilor Ar'Arith.

"I have found one. She is at the security desk." he states bruskly. "The other two walked out of the building." *Fuck, she is out of the building and the Senior Council has one of the other two?* Tan shares in my concern "Enlighten me, Captain, to what is going on there."

"I am sorry, Senior Council. One of the two that snuck out is our mate, sir," I inform him.

"You and Commander Bl'Wski have claimed a human?" He sounds almost horrified.

"Not fully, Sir," I confess. "But we are showing marks and felt her leave the building."

"I will deal with the female at the desk, you and your brother better find your mate before the traitors do." The com goes dead. I shrug and look to the beast that is the most esteemed Marine Commander.

"Commander, take your mate and the rest of the females to quarters now that your marine contingent is here."

Chapter Eighteen - Tet

We are all lead off the ship into a storeroom near the hanger bay. There is some kind of chemical leak in the ship, so we not only had to dock but evacuate the ship. Millie, Yaretzi, and I find an unattended back door in the store room. We are up for an adventure and have a way out from under our guard's nose.

"We need to stick together and protect each other," I tell the other ladies. "Remember, we don't want to be captured by the bad guys. Just want to get a feel for this station. Maybe, do some shopping. We will charge it to my mates!"

"You are crazy," Yaretzi says, but she is right there with me as we sneak out of the store room. "Let's get going. We only have a few hours before they figure out that we are gone...That is if we are lucky."

Millie is with us. A bit of a surprise given her timid nature, but not unwelcome either. She is rather cute with mousey brown hair and soft eyes. However, hearing about her stories makes me wonder what kind of tiger she really is. We head out carefully into the empty hallway. Do we know where we were going? Oh, Hell no we have no clue, but we *are* on an adventure. When we got to the end, we had to chose. "Which way?" Yaretzi asks.

"I don't know," I tell her. Millie reaches into the pocket of her pants and pulls out a quarter and hands it to Yaretzi.

"OK. Heads is to the right." She flips the coin., "It's tails." We head down the left hallway, looking for a door that might lead out into the main part of the station. Winding through the halls, we stop at a few doors only to find them locked or we can hear voices. Nope don't want to get caught. We can understand some of the voices thanks to the translators that the medics on the ship gave us. That will make it easier to navigate once we find a way out.

We keep slinking down this hallway and that, until we find a door that opens for us. Looking around, we see a lobby area and doors in front of us. There is a large desk area to the right with what looks to be an alien security guard.

Kelsey, where are you? Tet asks.

Scram! You buzzkill. I don't want to talk to either of you! I block both of them right then and there. They don't need to ruin our adventure.

Almost to the outside, we just need to cross the lobby without the guard stopping us.

"OK, we need to look like we are supposed to be here," Yaretzi softly says. "Just keep walking with purpose. We will worry about getting back in when we are done." We begin to stride through the lobby. Unfortunately, the tentacle guy notices us.

"Hey, I don't think you three should be in here!" He is yelling at us.

"Keep going, I will stall him," Yaretzi tells us in a whisper then loudly proclaims to the guard, "You are right!" Yaretzi does her best sashay to the guard as we hustle to the front door. This allows Millie and I to leave the lobby.

And then we are free! Well, kind of. In front of us is a large city. With buildings that reach up to an artificial sky. There are aliens all around and some don't look to savory, but I hold Millie's hand and stride forward like I have no reason to be afraid of any of these guys. I have walked through downtown at midnight without being molested, so I don't see this as a problem…I think.

My heart, we will meet you at the Galactic Gallery. I think you will enjoy shopping there. Tan reaches out and sends me the directions. *Tell them you are our mate and to put everything you want on our tab.*

What? Really? Well, that is a surprise.

Yes, my heart. My mother shops there anytime she visits the station with our fathers. Well, if it is good enough for my MIL. Oh, wow, I have a mother-in-law. What will she think of me?

She will love you as much as we do, my heart, Tet chimes in.

"Well, Millie, we have a destination!" I tell her and march through the streets of this intergalactic metropolis like a local.

Chapter Nineteen – Tan

So, we stay here temporarily or are they going to find us some place where we can rest?" Maryellen asks her beast of a mate. He just indicates to me. "Well?"

"We are working on secure housing," I say quickly. "Of course, you and your mate have a dwelling on the station due to Commander Max's rank and grade. However, the other women need to be kept safe. It is unfortunate that my mate chose this time to lead her fellow humans astray."

"Don't be too harsh on Kelsey," She tells me softly. "You know she really does have feelings for you and your brother. She told me so herself." I am surprised by this, as is my brother. "However, she is a free spirit, so you need to be a little less controlling with her."

"But we must keep her safe and teach her the duties of a mate to a command team," I tell her. She just nods sagely.

"Yes, you do need to keep her safe, but that doesn't mean to stifle her... natural exuberance." She smiles kindly. "Give her a little freedom, talk to her, and find out about who *she* is as a person and you might be surprised at how she will enhance your lives. If she truly is your true and fated mate then you may want to remember that she is a human and we need to see love, not just biological markings and orders."

My heart, we will meet you at the Galactic Gallery. I think you will enjoy shopping there, I tell her. *Tell them you are our mate and to put everything you want on our tab.*

What? Really? Kelsey is surprised by my generosity.

Yes, my heart. My mother shops there anytime she visits the station with our fathers.

"What just happened?" I ask out loud to Maryellen.

"Yaretzi told the guard that tried to delay them that they were going shopping." He then smirks. "On 'Kelsey's mates dime'. Kelsey and Millie escaped. Tet is not happy that I gave our mate directions to a trusted shop." A gasp escaped from her mouth. "I told her to have fun shopping and we will be there to pick her up when we are done."

"Good for you!" Her smile is broad. "She will appreciate that you trust her enough to give her that little bit of freedom."

His lips stretch in a beautiful smile. "She feels …happy."

"I bet she is," Maryellen confirms.

That is when my brother has Commander Max take the remaining females to their quarters.

Chapter Twenty - Kelsey

Millie and I are still having an adventure, but the city is large and a tad scary. Several males look at us with interest, but I give them my best bitch look. This keeps most of them at bay. A few try to detain us. I just look at them and say, "No thanks, I am meeting my mates somewhere and they won't appreciate having to clean your carcass off their boots. Tet and Tan are a bit possessive." That generally gets them to step back and let us pass.

Just like males on Earth, women have to invoke the mate, husband, or boyfriend to get them to back off. Seriously, why can't females throughout the Universe just walk around without males trying to molest them. Just take "no" for an answer, assholes.

Just as I start worrying I may be lost a big sign over a fancy shop that says, *The Galactic Gallery.* Holy shit, this is some fancy shop. Where did my mates send me?

Millie and I walk in the door and a green female with shiny black hair hanging down her back, horns, and pointed ears towers over us as she greets us. "Ladies, what can I do for you? Such a surprise to have humans enter my establishment." She looks us up and down, but her smile doesn't leave. I am a little uncomfortable. Anytime my mom and I were in stores like this one, we had just had a trip to get our nails and hair done and were dressed to the nines. Millie and I barely ran combs through our hair and our clothes are what the replicator could make, not real stylish.

"My mates, Tet and Tan Bl'Wski, told me to meet them here." I try to be cool.

"Tenaya Bl'Wski's sons? Well, welcome, we are privileged to have the mate of her oldest sons. Will you excuse me, please. Take a look around and I will be back to assist you." Well, maybe, we won't have that "Pretty Woman" moment. Millie and I enjoy going through some of the displays. They don't have racks of clothes like stores on Earth. Instead, there are holographic mannequins that move to show you the outfit. They talk to you and tell you that you might like it in a different color or need these accessories to go with the garments. Truly interactive.

We are having so much fun. Then it happened, the green female returns.

"I am sorry, humans, but Tenaya says her sons have no mate." She looks upset, but still maintains a professional demeanor. "I am going to have to regretfully ask you to leave."

"But my mates are meeting me here!" I state.

Tet must have felt my panic. *What is the matter, my heart.*

The lady says that your mother doesn't know me and I have to leave. I let him know. Suddenly, the green alien's com goes off. I hear Tet sternly talking to the female. All we hear clearly is her murmurs of, "Yes, Sir.", "I understand, Sir." And, finally, "Anything they want, yes, Sir." She looks at me with embarrassment.

"I am terribly sorry, My Lady." I feel a bit sorry for her. She was polite and let us look around. But I am also glad I have a telepathic mate that could lay into her, because I had no clue what we would have done, if we had to leave. "It is okay., I assure her. "You didn't know. Heck, my mother-in-law didn't know. This is a very new relationship, you see. We" I indicate to Millie and I, "Were just rescued a week ago from these creepy slaver dudes." She looks a bit relieved and starts showing us clothing that we would need if we plan on staying on the space station.

We are on our way; have some fun, my heart, Tan states.

We apologize. We should have contacted mother and let her know we had found you. Tet is feeling bad for the situation.

It is OK, the lady was professional and very nice, I reassured them. Really, at no time was she mean, even when she thought we had lied.

"My mates are on their way. We will enjoy looking around on our own but thank you for being so kind. Despite the mix up." She quickly leaves us to our own devices but stays close in case we need anything. I found a few outfits that looked comfortable and the owner came to show me how to order. The dress was made in just seconds and it was a perfect fit. I asked about undergarments and she showed me their lingerie. Within moments I had a whole new wardrobe. Millie was hesitant to let my mates buy her clothes, but she was convinced to let me order her a few new outfits.

By the time Tet and Tan roll in, there is quite a large pile of boxes ready to be shipped to our quarters.

I throw my arms around Tet and give him a quick kiss before doing the same for Tan. They chuckle as they look at the pile.

You had a good time didn't you, my heart? Tet puffs out his chest in pride.

Yes, my mate, I acquiesce to him with a quick hug. *You don't mind that I bought so much?*

No, my heart, this won't force bankruptcy on Tet and I Tan gives me a wink.

"My lords, your mate has done you proud." The green female is almost bowing in her obeisance, "Like your mother, she has excellent taste."

"I am glad that she has something in common with our mother, A'Gam," Tan says with a grin.

"Is there a hair dresser and nail salon nearby," I ask knowing full well I am pushing the gambit a bit, but I must look a fright next to the elegant female. "I must look a fright after so much time on board a ship full of males who have no clue what it takes to keep a woman pretty." I feel my mates humor.

"Actually, you will like this, Lady Bl'Wski!" She has me step into a booth, there is an image on the wall that confirms my statement. A few moments with some soothing energy and my curls are shiny and bouncy. My face is beautifully made up and my nails look like works of art. A'Gam handed me one of my more casual outfits and…*Voilà!* I look like I just stepped out of a sleek shop on Rodeo Drive. Tet and Tan give me hot looks as I leave the booth.

"Common, Millie. Your turn." I grab my friend and shove her into the booth with a new outfit. When she walks out of the booth, she is gorgeous.

"Oh Millie, you are beautiful!" She shines with confidence. "Now, you just stay away from my males." I tell her with a big grin, but I am a bit concerned. She really is so beautiful.

There is nothing for you to worry about, Kelsey, Tan reassures me, *You are the only female we will ever want.*

Tan is correct, Tet confirms. *After having you, we can never want or need another.*

"Now, my heart, it is time to head back the Council Building." Tet give A'Gam a stern, "Please have my mate and her friend's packages sent to our quarters. While I am pleased that you treated my mate with respect, even when you doubted who she was, you should have called my brother and I, not our mother."

"Yes, Sir." She turns to me, "I am sorry, My Lady."

"It is fine really. It could have been much worse," I tell her. "On Earth, we have a story that is about a girl who is treated poorly by shopgirls who think she is not the right sort. You didn't ever treat us like that, you didn't look down your nose at us or treat us as less than, even when you asked us to leave. It says lot about your character."

"I would hope I never judge anyone that harshly. I just asked Teyana, because she was in a few days ago and didn't mention the mating. But I do see the error." A'Gam looks at my mates, " I hope I didn't get you in trouble with your mother, my lords."

"Not too much," Tet states. "Our mother is on her way here now to meet our mate. She just got back to Akkadia and will leave tomorrow after she checks on her business."

"Now, I am concerned," I state. Their mother is on her way. What will she think of me? What will I think of her? What if she hates me?

She will love you, Tet reassures me.

We bid farewell to A'Gam and head out into the street. As we head back, Millie and I feel much better. Tet and Tan scowl at any male that looks twice at us. Who knew I would appreciate having two such scary men protecting me?

We did, they say in tandem and smugly.

Shit, I really need to block them if I want to keep my thoughts my own.

Chapter Twenty-One – Ab'Nel

Commander…I mean, Captain" Well, that is interesting…I wonder where that came from though I suspect I know. "Report, Gin'Gie." I demand.

"Sir, Captain Schnel'Dn is dead. The mission was discovered too quickly and the team didn't have enough time to leave with the product."

"What happened to Schnel'Dn?" I ask. I suppose I will need to add that to the report.

"He tried to take a youngling from a human mated to a Caeterin." Gin'Gie hesitates, "The Caeterin went into beast mode and tore him to pieces, Sir." That doesn't surprise me. The Captain got greedy and was just too stupid to live. The youngling of a Caeterin mate? He obviously knew she was mated and what she was mated to. "Sir, do you want the body vid?"

"I guess I need it." So, I am now Captain. Well, there are some things I will need to do. "Gin'Gie?"

"Yes, Comm…Captain."

"You are now first mate. Get back to the bridge." I tell him, "There are things that I need to do and I will need a commander I at can trust." Oh, I don't trust him in the least, but he is better than any of the other males on this ship.

"Yes, Sir! Thank you, Sir!"

With that I head to Schnel'Dn's quarters to see what he didn't want his family to see before his brother vetted it. Before going there, I stop in the office to pull the chip from behind the panel. I place it in the reader after I secure the office. Schnel'Dn's voice booms out of the desk com.

"Well, my boy, you are now Captain. Hopefully, because I am now retired. If not, I am dead. You have my instructions for that unfortunate event." I don't know if it is unfortunate, but alright I guess, "Anyway, you are the Captain of this ship and now, privy to the secrets of our benefactors. You need to head to H'Atar and meet with head of the An Ratha family. My boy, you will be in shock when you meet with them. But keep your head and you will find a way to make this opportunity fully payout for you." Interesting... he was working with one of the biggest crime families in the Twelve galaxies. No wonder, he thought he would retire and worked to get those humans recaptured. Well, I guess I know what I need to do.

"Gin'Gie, set a course to H'Atar. Keep the cloaking on until we enter that system." He confirms and I head to Schnel'Dn's quarters. Now, let see what a truly sick fuck he was.

Chapter Twenty-Two – Kelsey

B ut why haven't you claimed her yet, my sons?" This is my new "mother-in-law". "You don't want other males to swoop in and claim this beautiful gem. I want grand younglings!" She hugs me like I am her favorite toy and they better do what she wants. I do like how she has taken to me, but I can barely breathe with her smothering me.

I could see both of my mates in the eyes of their mother and the set of their chins. The last few days had been tough. While we continued to have incredible sex, when not in the throws of passion they kept me a virtual prisoner and it chaffed my butt to be curtailed so much and I was ready to march out and leave them, but their mother was a surprise. I was expecting a stuck up, grand dame, but she is neither. She, also, was several inches taller than me, rail-thin and had her white hair cut in a sophisticated bob with her elf ears dripping jewelry.

"That is my fault…Ma'am." I struggle to say. She looks at me with surprise, like I popped out of a big birthday cake.

"Your fault! Oh no, my sweet child, they did it." She wags her finger at my mates as she drags me to a lounger and forces me to sit. "They have always been so stiff and boring. I am surprised to see you stick around and not run away from them." Both Tet and Tan have scowls on their faces.

My heart, our mother can be a bit bothersome, Tan says, then Tet agreed, *Tell us if you need us to send her home*

"Let me guess. They are telling you that I am overbearing and inappropriate?" I giggle-snorted at her correct statement.

"They do have sticks up their asses and that is why I haven't let them claim me." She gasps with a merry twinkle in her eyes. My mates were horrified as I continue. "I haven't decided if I can put up with all their rules and regulations for the rest of my life and it would be a very long life if they are to be believed."

"Oh, I love that! Yes, they do have 'sticks up their asses', just like their fathers." She laughs at the shocked looks on their faces. "I almost didn't mate with Fade and Fen, because of that very same issue! But when they weren't being overbearing *arnackles,* they were lovely, kind and made me feel sooo good, with wiggling eyebrows, "so, so good."

"Mother!" Both males yelled out. She just waved their outrage away.

"And that is why I haven't run screaming from them." I wink back. "So good."

Remember you are talking to our mother, my heart, Tan sounded positively scandalized and that is a trick with telepathy.

"I am sorry, Lady Bl'Wski, if I overstepped my boundaries." I looked contrite.

"First off, to you I am Tayana." She smiles at me. "Secondly, I am very well aware what goes on between males and females, so don't mind the rambling thoughts of my younglings. I mean, they and their siblings wouldn't be here if it wasn't for lots of good mating." She started laughing at the sheer disgust on her sons' faces. I guess it doesn't matter where in the Universe you are, children never want to acknowledge that their parents have sex, not the least have it confirmed by their mothers affirming the joy of it.

Our mother goes too far, Tet says with a feeling of indignation.

Oh no, she may be the only reason I decide to let you claim me, I think back cheekily. *So, you best be nice to her.*

We love our mother, but I worry that she will be a bad influence on you, Tan replies testily.

Maybe she hopes I will be a good influence on you, I give them the side eye.

"My sons, I think you should talk to your fathers." Tayana states with a look that brooked no nonsense from the big males. She has a big smile on her face as she turns to me. "You, my dear, are exactly what these two need. I don't want them to screw this up because they can't remember what it means to have a little fun in life. I tried to remind them of this when they were young, but their fathers were always about rules and duty. If you decide to take them on, know that I will back you up."

She turned to my mates. "You will talk to your fathers when they arrive tomorrow evening. I think it will surprise you to learn a few things, and I know, it will stick better coming from them." She rose from her seat and stepped toward the door. "I am going to head to my quarters and take a nap. I will return this evening to take my new daughter out for some fun! I can't imagine that you two have thought to take her to explore the joys of this station, have you?"

"It is not safe to take a human out into the space station until she is mated," Tet tries to weasel his way out of his mother's condemnation.

"Well then, *YOU* can escort us, but *I* am taking her out to see something other than you two." With that Tayana plants a kiss on each of their cheeks and is out the door and gone.

"I really like your mother," I say with a smirk.

She is chaotic, but our fathers adore their mate, Tan is reflective.

She is amazing and I adore her already. I tell them. Tet gets a smile on his face.

I think our mate is a lot like our mother, Tan muses. I start laughing at that thought.

Human males often marry women like their moms, I muse. *Maybe, Akkadianans do, too.* Then I give them a look as I turn and sashay to the bedroom. *I am taking a nap. I suspect your mother will run us ragged tonight.* I call back and next thing I know, they are joining me. I guess I won't be getting much of a nap after all.

Chapter Twenty–Three – Tet

Kelsey, remember, there is nothing more fun than spending my mates' money, unless it is spending my sons' money! They are all so tight until I am the one to go shopping!"

My mother laughs merrily as she and Kelsey walk before us. I had suspected that going out with my mother was a dangerous occupation and I was right, but not because of the dangers on the Council Station. No, my mother brings chaos wherever she goes, and today that chaos appears to be with Tan and my credits. We follow her and our mate as they trot through the Council Station's Shopping District. The pile of purchases are sent to our quarters thankfully. Though, maybe, if we are carrying them, my mother or our mate would take pity on us and end this excursion.

"Mother, we don't need to buy a bunch of useless things. The military provides us with all our needs." I try to use logic.

You know that isn't going to work. Tan looks at me.

"Tan, you know I can feel yours and your brother's frustration, but it will do you no good. I know that this sweet human needs a lot more from you than just basics if you plan on mating her," Mother admonishes both of us. Then giggles. "I need more daughters and I like Kelsey," She squeezes our mate. Who turns a lovely shade of pink.

Honest guys, this is the most shopping I have ever done, your mother is a pro! Kelsey seems a bit ill at ease with all the credits we are spending.

Don't worry, my heart, I assure her, *We have plenty of credits, despite what our mother may indicate to the contrary. If we can't afford it, we will tell you, but for now, you have hardly put a dent into the credits we have saved up.*

Mother finally lets us stop to eat at one of the trendy eateries on the Council Station. A bistro that specializes in pairing Mitirian wines with different cuisines from around the fifteen systems.

"Now, your fathers are due in tomorrow. They were asked to be at that council meeting; I assume you will be there too?" Both of us nod.

"Council meeting?" Kelsey asks. "What Council meeting?"

"The Galactic Federation Council is meeting to discuss the situation with galaxy H495, solar system J2695, we know it as G348," I say to calm her. I admit that I purposefully chose to use the planetary designation.

I know you are talking about Earth, and I wonder why neither of you told me your Counsel is discussing my planet, she looks at me pointedly then says, "I should like to be there. Is the meeting an open meeting for the public?" Before I can say 'No," my mother answers for me.

"Yes, Dear. You should be there!" Mother gives me that "you are trying to hide something" look, before turning to Kelsey. "I find those meetings so terribly dull, but my mates will be there to support you and your human friends."

"What about my planet are they discussing?" My mate looks at Tan and I with a similar look to my mother.

We will be discussing the security situation and how to discourage more abductions of human females, Tan states.

"Tan, darling. Mother can't hear your voice, but I feel you are saying something. I miss hearing your voice in my head, my child." She sighs. "I guess you have just grown up and let that part go." When we joined the military, they taught us to sever the link with our parents, for our safety and theirs.

"Mother, please," My brother growls out. "I was just explaining that the meeting will be about securing G348."

"You mean Earth, right?" Our mate clarifies. "You should use 'Earth' if that is what you mean. We are more than a number. I am sure you don't call your planets by their designation numbers?"

"Yes, my heart," Tan acquiesces. "We should use 'Earth' Now that we know what your planet has been named by its people."

I am sure if you showed me the star charts, I could tell you the numbers humans use for you. She giggles a bit as Tan looks at her and growls. "I just reminded him that you folks aren't the only ones with number designations for planets," She informs my mother, causing another round of giggles as my mother snorts inelegantly.

Dinner continues on at a leisurely pace. Kelsey and mother sharing more stories of our families. I am saddened to think that Kelsey doesn't think her parents would notice her disappearance. I know that I would notice her missing. I would do everything in my power to find her should she go missing. My heart squeezes in fear at the very thought. I have to acknowledge that my mate means everything to me.

Chapter Twenty-Four – Ab'Nel

My lady, there is a Misagian here to see you." I could hear the timid little male through the door as I waited in a cold room with no windows.

⌐end the captain in." A harsh female voice sighs.

"Um…m…my l…lady," the small man stutters, "I…it isn't the s…same c…captain that you know, my lady".

"What? Who is it?" She sounds powerful "Oh…Blast it all… Show the fool in and I will ascertain why this one has come." I will show this female that I am not a fool.

"Yes, my lady." The obsequious little male comes and directs me in. This female must be powerful. I stride into the room and there she is. She is not large, but she projects power. I drink it in like mother's milk. She is magnificent. Not beautiful by the standards of my people, but I sense the need to keep this female in my life.

"You're a female." I say with the disbelief. Upon seeing how this female makes me feel, I am struck with the realization, she is my mate. Ugly as her species is, I know this, and she is not a beauty by any standard; triangular head topped by dark green hair that is scraped back in a knot on the top of her head. I suspect that hair is her best feature. Her eyes are round and buggy. She has two arms that end in three clawed fingers and eight tentacles that protrude from her back. *I best keep an eye on those, unless they are around my dick…* Probably even then, if I want to keep it.

"Yes, yes, I am a female," She looks at me with sharp eyes. "The real question is *who* are *you* and what are you doing here?" She thinks I don't know that the politeness is a ruse. "I mean that I have only one Misagian captain that I do business with and you are not him, so I assume something has gone wrong with the mission he was sent on?"

"Yeeeesss." I assess the room around me. She does have power. However, I will be the power over her.

"You need to quit looking," she says like she thinks she knows me. "There will be no males coming to do business with you. I am the head of the An Ratha family. Were you not informed?"

"Um, no, my lady." I use the polite title, but I don't feel polite. I continue my perusal of the room, "There were no instructions about *who* we were doing business with. Just that I was to come here and report to the head of the An Ratha."

"Who gave you these orders?" There is a quirk to her thin lips. She will be sucking my cock when I am done with her, but for now, let her think she is the power here.

"It was in an encoded data file left by Captain Schnel'Dn to be delivered to me, his second-in-command and first cousin, upon his death," I inform her.

"So, he is dead? What happened?" She asks.

"He went with our men to take the females that had been lured off the *Patience* when our inside personnel had sabotaged the life support. The mission was almost a success, but my idiot cousin…I mean…Captain Schnel'Dn…" I correct myself, but I can tell she likes my impudence, "Chose to try and take the youngling of an already mated female. She called out and her…her…her mate, a Caeterin in beast form, burst through the door and annihilated all the personnel within the storeroom.

"So, my cargo was not retrieved?" she asks with an edge to her voice.

"No, my lady." I show my anger at the stupidity. "None of the cargo was retrieved at that time. We didn't even get the bodies of our personnel back. Our planet's leaders were questioned by the Council and they, the cowards, said to ship the bodies to the nearest sun. They didn't even ask for genetic material to identify them." I am overcome with the needless loss of my crewmates. "It was left to me to contact the families of the dead personnel and provide their shares to them."

"How did you know what happened?" she asks as though she cares, but I know better. She is my mate and her money and power will be mine.

"Each of our personnel had live video cams on their armor. The bridge personnel monitored the action on a secured line. Each body that fell, the signal cut off and the cam had a needle that expelled a poison as it self-destructed to make sure the personnel could not be healed and used as a witness against us I designed the cam myself." She looks impressed with my safeguards.

"And you have personnel amongst the council?" Oh, she is thinking of how to use me. I will need to hold my credits close to my chest, so she doesn't steal them.

"No, not the council, but some of their Gurtanian guards are on our pay." I let her think she is humoring me. She and her powerful family will be under *my* control.

"And what about repayment of the cargo your personnel lost?" Interesting that she should bring this up; she still thinks my men will waste time on this. I have a better plan.

"You have no males to do these negotiations?" I query.

"They were all killed by the Galactic Federation forces." Stating the fact with little emotion, "But I am perfectly capable of taking care of my family and negotiating in their best interests."

"It is not right for a female to head a business enterprise such as this." I love how her spine straightens.

"Well, one does what one has to, when there is a need." She is intrigued by me. I can read this female like a book. I step in closer to her, while watching her carefully. One wrong move and she will attack.

"Tell me, my lady." I look into those dark orbs though still a few feet away. "Can you still breed?"

"That is very personal, Captain… I'm sorry but I don't even know your name." Oh, yes, she is intrigued.

"Schnel'Kal. Ab'nel Schnel'Kal…" I give her my name like a taunt. "Now, answer my question, my lady."

"Well, I suppose I could still…breed. I was the youngest of my mother's hatchlings and my oldest youngling was only twenty seasons," she tells me. Yes, she will do nicely for what I need.

"Here is my proposition. I need a mate and I don't want one of those overbred females on my planet." I don't tell her she is my mate as I begin, "You need a male to head your organization." I move even closer. "I have half of our personnel's stipends that had been saved. The rest I sent to their families as death payments. That left a large amount for me to purchase a mate. But as I said, you need a male, and I need a mate. So, I will mate with you and you will be given the rest of the stipend as a 'mate payment'. Then *I* will become the face of this organization."

"You think *I* am going to turn all this over to *you*?" She is not playing now. I have her. "You can't even negotiate a bath!" Ah, she is the reason for that unholy habit of Schnel'Dn's. Well, for power, sacrifices must be made but for now, she needs to learn. I grab her quickly, making sure to catch all her tentacles and trap them against my body, before she can use them against me.

"You will be my mate and will give me sons." One arm holds around the abdomen while the other has her by the neck. I whisper in her audial holes, "Our hybrids will be powerful and we will rule the Universe." She tries to slide her tentacles from under me. "Ah ah ah, You are not going to get away from me that easily, female. I have determined that you are mine. You are strong and cunning. I need this in a mate. You come with large holdings with fingers all over eight galaxies. I can overlook that you are not from an attractive species, but I know we will breed interesting young that will expand our empire. You might even enjoy it. I know I will." I slip my hand to her cunt… it is mine, as she gasps and she is mine. I know this when she slips a tentacle over my turgid erection, "Oh, yeah, I will definitely enjoy you."

"I will mate you per your proposal on a few non-negotiable conditions," she purrs. "One, you will sign all property in your name, to me. I am not going to hand over my empire, just to have it stolen by a presumptuous male. Two, you will let me bath you every day, so that I don't have to deal with the smell of you and you will let me make you presentable. I don't want my business associates to be disgusted by your look and smell." I smell bad? What is she talking about? I smell like most Misagian males. "Do you agree?"

"You mean bathe in water?" I am not too sure, but I may have to sacrifice for the power I will have.

"Yes, with a strong soap." She is really trying to make a point.

"I see the logic in turning over my holdings to you, so if I die, my family can't go after it. However, the bathing seems unreasonable." I have to try.

"Your cousin didn't seem to mind." She looks at me meaningfully.

"My cousin was an idiot." I really am beginning to see that I will definitely need to sacrifice.

"Come with me," she says in a low sultry voice. I let her slip from my arms and lead me to a room with a large tub full of water. Swirling water with a sweet scent is enticing.

We enjoy each other as we fight for control. I penetrate her, pumping her full of my seed. A feeling I had never felt before overtook me. I will tolerate baths where I can fuck my mate, ugly as she is. I already am in love with her tight cunt. She will brood my young. I will make sure of that. I will fill her with so much seed she won't have time to threaten me and when I bit her, she knew my death was hers. We are mates and will stay that way until death. May it be a good match for us and for our business, an unholy alliance blessed by the gods.

Chapter Twenty-Five - Kelsey

I walk with my males boxing me in between them. I admit that their presence soothes me. Looking through the large, intimidating room is a tad scary for me. It is like I really am not supposed to be here, but I keep reminding myself that I am needed here to speak for my planet and all those billions of people who don't know what is out her, away from our tiny solar system.

Continuing my perusal of the room, I start to see my friends and I wave to them. Tet and Tan have me so sandwiched that this filling isn't going anywhere without them. They sit us towards the front next to two more identical males who look similar to my mates. Tet introduces the older males as their fathers, Fen and Fade Bl'Wski. They give a mild smile of acknowledgement then turn forward again to pay attention to the dais. Tet and Tan seem like good little soldiers taking the same position as their fathers. Sitting at attention but "at ease" as they wait for the meeting to start. I just look around the rest of the room. Amazed at all the different beings who filled the auditorium.

"That is the council?" I indicate to the dais with fourteen beings all dressed in beautiful robes. My mates acknowledge that, yes, they are the Council. I just look on with curiosity. There are only two females. One looks ok, like a kindly yellow granny with a red feather hat, except the hat is growing from her head. The other looks like a bitch, an ugly bitch... an insect-y, ugly bitch... Yeah, I just bet she has a beautiful spirit, despite her nasty ass looks. OK, I am being a bit shallow, but she really looks mean.

Cara called out to Maryellen, then she saw me and waves without a call Millie, Winona, and Victoria sit with her. Winona and Millie wave back as I silently greet them from my position. Victoria looks at my mates then me with an eyebrow up and her lips pursed in disapproval. I am tempted to climb on Tet's lap and lean over to make out with Tan, just to shock the prude, but I remember that this is neither the time nor place to start trouble. I represent Earth and need to try and be on my best behavior

Just as we are settling in and waiting for the center seat to be taken on the dais, a loud ruckus starts up at the entryway. First, a tall male, turquoise with lavender hair and horns coming out of his head, strides in followed by big males that look like mutant bulldogs. A tiny, or at least compared to all those males, human female angrily struts into the room. I almost didn't recognize my friend, Yaretzi, as she was dressed in a luxurious robe, her hair and make-up done to perfection.

Oh, good, the Senior Council is here. Tet thought. *But…is that?*

Yep, that is Yaretzi, I respond. *Doesn't she look so beautiful?*

No one is as beautiful as you, my heart, Tan answers.

Nice save, but, seriously, she really is looking gorgeous. I am adamant.

I will acquiesce to your judgment, Tet looks seriously at me, *Tan and I can only see you, our mate. The most beautiful female of all and that is how it will be for our whole lives. You are all we have and will ever desire.* Tan just stares at me with those amazing eyes. They really know how to make me have all those feels. Though this wasn't a test, they would have passed with flying colors had it been… I guess they really do like me.

Yes, my heart. Tet smiles at me. *We more than like you. I don't know what this "test" is, but we will do anything to have you say "yes" to claiming by us.*

For a moment my eyes are captured in their gaze. Then Yaretzi starts yelling. "I am not your *puta!*" The big male leans and says something to her in a low voice. I don't know what he is saying, I'm just too far away from them, but Yaretzi isn't happy. If she had a knife in her hand, he would be bleeding. Instead, she puts her middle finger in his face with a false smile. He stands tall, turns and walks to the dais to take his seat in the middle of the Galactic Federation Council. His face is a mask of stoicism.

The Senior Council does not look happy. Tet observed. *Maybe, he has discovered what trouble human mates can be?* He muses.

Oh, I have been easy on you two. I smirk at him. I so admire Yaretzi's style, such an elegant flip off.

Don't make me spank you, my heart. Tan gives me some serious side eye.

MMMMMmmm, threatening me with a good time, I feel him straighten and look sternly at me. I just look up at him and flutter my lashes with a coy smile.

My heart, I just don't know what to do with you. Tet smiles a bemused smile as he watches the proceedings.

Very simple, don't try to change me, and I won't try to change you. With that I go back to paying attention. Not that it was easy, lots of posturing by the council members about this budget and that invoice…A variance granted to Caeterin this thingamajig… Mittras gets that doohickey… blah, blah, blah…

My heart, if you want to go back to our quarters, I will escort you, Tan tells me.

Nice try, but no, I need to be here for now, I reply. *I am trying to not show my boredom, now quit distracting me.*

You are doing quite well, my heart. Tet sends a wave of affection through our connection. *I didn't know you could act so well. Only Tan and I know how bored you are because we feel it. All others…*

"And now, we come to the planet in galaxy H495, solar system J2695. We know it as G348." The Senior Council announces the next agenda item, "The locals call it Earth and themselves humans. The Galactic Federation is in quandary, because while we have banned ships from the Federation and its subsidiaries from entering that solar system…" The Senior Council was interrupted by the door opening, by a big man of the same species as him and a beautiful and obviously pregnant human with a big smile on her face enter. I am struck by the couple. He looks a lot like the Senior Council, yet he is bigger and bulkier than the male that claims Yaretzi.

"Hail, cousin! Am I late for the festivities?" Shouting shamelessly, the big male just smiles at the dour Senior Council.

"We were just getting started, D'Artimus." The Senior Council looks about ready to laugh but he holds himself together. "Please find a seat for your mate. That youngling she carries has to be a great burden for such a dainty creature." Many smile at her as a less than dainty snort rings out through the room. They make a move towards Rin'On and Maryellen. We watch as the couples greet each other until there is a collective harrumph from the dais.

"If we can continue," the Senior Council begins again with the line item that is on his agenda. "Now, with G348, also known as Earth, we are finding that for the past 5-6 galactic years, the rate of humans, particularly human females, within our designated space has increased ten fold." He looks over at Yaretzi and the very pregnant woman next to Maryellen. He shakes his head, "As charming as these sentient beings are, we can not allow a primitive species like these humans be victims of slavers and pirates who have decided they are fair game."

Who's he calling primitive? I am not good with that title, *We may not be advanced technologically, but we are hardly primitive.*

My heart, it is merely a designation of your technology, Tet consoles me. *Not your intelligence.*

However, with a mate like his, maybe he is looking at the civilization? I jab Tan with my elbow at that dig. He gives a token grunt with a sly smile.

The female council member with the bug face gets all on her high horse, "Why should we get involved with such a puny species? If anything, they are being helped by being allowed to learn from civilized species. I, also, don't even see the appeal of these tiny creatures."

If your males have females as ugly as you, you are just jealous, I think.

Now, my heart, be kind. The males of her kind are even uglier, Tet replies. Oh, that got me. I put my head down to hide my silent giggles.

"Well, that is easy for an H'Atari to say," The big bull dog looking Councilmember says. "They have a plethora of females to give their males sons. Most of our members are barely hanging on, with our populations dwindling as our females produce more males to females."

"Well, my lord councilmember from Gurtania, can we help that our clutches are three to five eggs. Our fertility is legendary." Wow, is she a bitch or what… and she lays eggs…ick.

The sweet little granny with the plumage on her head cuts in, "Now, now, let's remain civilized as you claim we are, More'll. I would like to talk to the humans that I see before us."

"I have no objections." The Senior Council approves, "D'Artimus bring your mate and the other humans up here." Before I finish jumping out of my seat to head forward, my mates are there, guiding me forward. Michelle is being escorted by a huge purple male who is looking downright annoyed to be here, but like my guys, he doesn't let her go far without him. As we get to the space in front of the long dais, the males all give a salute with their hands to their chests and their heads bowing.

Then the sweet little old lady starts. "My, my. There are a lot of you here today and look…a youngling. What is your name, little one?"

"I am Jaycee and I am four yearth old. Would you like to see my looth tooth?" Maryellen's cute little girl, Jaycee, steps forward, but her mother keeps her from going to far.

"I would love to see your loose tooth, my lady Jaycee," then the councilmember does an aside to her, "But I think we should wait until this very boring meeting is over."

"OK, nice lady, after dis boring meeting. But it isn't that boring because the people are so cool, with all their beautiful colors and *you* have feathers!" The councilmember is charmed by the human child.

Of course, Bugface McBitchyface cuts into the amusing interaction. "Why are we being bothered with this youngling? In a Council meeting of all places."

"Because it is her planet and the home of millions like her that you are discussing, Councilmember Tri'Acrera?," Maryellen goes all momma bear. "She has just as much right as any of us."

"None of you primitives have a right to be here," the bitch counters. "It is just the Senior Council bowing to his cousin and, I think," Pointing to Yaretzi. "His mate! This is not appropriate at all. Highly irregular. None of you females are members of the Galactic Federation and it is an abomination that, at least, two of you look to be bearing young off these males! Disgusting!"

Oooo, nose holes flaring...I don't think she likes humans, I think.

H'Atari don't like anyone that isn't under their power, Tet tells me.

Or they owe money too. Tan smirks while I lower my head and eyes to hide my amusement.

"Councilmember, your distaste is not shared by many on this council," a large purple councilmember states. "Please refrain from such outbursts as they reflect badly on this august body. Commander O'Jectic, I see you have escorted a human here." Michelle's big purple guy grumpily pulls her closer to him.

"Yes, my lord," He growls.

"Is she your mate?" Michelle seems shocked by the question.

"Oh, haillll no!" she states in that Southern drawl. "This asshole is driving me up a wall and you think he wants to mate with me?"

"I have not claimed her as yet, my lord," he growls again. The councilmember smirks as Michelle looks on with shock.

"Well, you best get her in line, Commander." The big male states and several of us start to bristle when Rin'On chimes in.

"My lords and ladies, one does not just claim a human mate," Rin'On addresses the Council and the audience. "Human mates are wonderful for those of us lucky enough to find her. However, they are a species that doesn't feel their mates, like many of us do. They ahhh…" His wife…mate, whatever…takes pity on him and begins explaining about how human women fall in love.

She continues to expound on the ways of courting a human ending with a bit of a censure "…After the abduction and subsequent rescue, I have learned that I have a fated mate, who is devoted not only to me, but to my child…I mean youngling. He even rescued me from an attacker who wanted to steal my baby and sell her! Sell my child…a four year old youngling! What kind of Galactic Federation allows such scum to exist?"

"So, you call us scum now, you primitive?" Mr. Stinky McGreasy, the species that ran the slave ship we woke on, is on the Council.

"Only if you allow these abductions to continue!" Maryellen is taking no prisoners. "I am not asking you to initiate first contact. Just allow Galactic Federation ships to patrol the solar system as discreetly as possible and protect humans from those who would prey on my people. As you say, we are not big and strong…well, by your standards. I am a giant compared to most human females… We need that protection and if your esteemed colleague from …" Her mate gives her the planet name… H'Atar, sounds like you are hocking a loogie, "H'Atar is correct in saying we don't belong here, then maybe, protecting our planet from these criminals will help to reduce the number of humans taken."

"I hate to say this, my lady," the council member that looks a lot like my mates begins to speak, "But there appears to be a need for human females. Looking at you and your mate, I see that Caeterins are compatible with humans and, as much as Hontor wants to deny it, it looks like you humans are compatible with them," He looks right at me. "What about you, female. I see two of our finest warriors stand with you?"

"I haven't let them claim me yet," I state.

"Why not?" The male stares at me in wonder, then he looks at the male standing in the back. Another set of twins.

"I just started dating them a few weeks ago. I want to make sure this truly is for life." I just don't know what to say, but I continue, "Besides… Oh, I don't know. I have never felt like this and it is scary."

We are here for you, my heart, Tet tells me as he and Tan move closer. I feel protected, but I continue. "Also, you do realize that girls on my planet get called all kinds of nasty names for having two mates?" this startles the council member and his twin, "Just because it is normal for your culture, doesn't make it normal for mine."

"As you can see, Councilmembers." The pregnant woman, Elizabeth, starts, her voice loud and clear, "Humans are complex creatures, and we don't get hints from the Universe that we are with the right person…being…whatever." She attempts to wrap her arms around her big male, but her belly gets in the way. "You are correct in thinking that your fertility problems might be solved by the introduction of human females, but you will need to tackle that another way. I am a fated mate, and I am blooming with a Hontoran/human baby. Boy…am I blooming." Gesturing to her distended stomach, "and we know that Rin'On and Maryellen are fated mates who are having a baby in the next solar."

"Could only be five months" Maryellen says with a smile on her face.

"Seriously?" She hits her mate, "You and your fifteen months gestation!" The Senior Council smirks. "Don't laugh, I hear you have a human mate! I feel sorry for her." I notice that Yaretzi smirks then. "But I digress, have any of these slaves been fertile? Have you even done studies? Is there a rise in the number of hybrid younglings being born in the Federation?"

"We don't know, Lady Elizabeth," the Senior Council speaks. "We have not noticed populations rising in any significant way."

"So," our human spokesperson continues to argue, "Smugglers are selling these humans with a promise of fertility and there isn't any proof of breeding success among unmated humans? So, they are swindlers and the humans are not their only victims."

"It would appear so," Cat faced councilmember states, "Studies should be done and, in the meantime, we should allow our ships to patrol in Solar System J2695 in stealth mode to discourage trafficking of Human females. We should, also, study the humans who have mated to see if they all become pregnant or only those mated to certain species… As an aside, Commander Max, congratulations. Your mating gives our species hope of survival."

"But Councilmember, sir," Cara starts. "How can it give hope if you won't let humans be a part of this Federation y'all are proud of?"

"That is a good question, female, and we will need to study this issue thoroughly. However, we can still celebrate the successful mating of my cousin." Oh, Maryellen looked a bit shocked by that announcement.

The council members continued to argue about what, if anything was needed in our sector of the Universe, as well as the need for fertile females.

I hope they aren't going to start letting those creeps abduct women. I am worried about what desperate males might do to keep their species alive.

They won't stoop that low, Tan assures me. *At least, most won't. Obviously, some of our member worlds are not truly honorable.*

The council came up with a resolution to study the matter of human compatibility with the various member species while allowing a battlegroup to patrol Earth's solar system and surrounding space for illegal activities by member species. Only two members voted against the resolution… Kind of easy to guess, huh? … Yep, the creepy guy and the bug bitch…

Chapter Twenty-Six – Tet

Tan and I sit with our fathers after the council meeting. We have brought our mate back to our quarters, only to find our mother there ready to swoop in and take our mate away.

"Have a nice chat with your fathers, my dear boys!" she cheerily calls as she takes our mate off to who knows where. Both Tan and I made an attempt to grab our mate away from our mother when my father, Fade, put his hand on my arm. He sighs then says, "Your mother will not allow any harm to come to your mate."

"No, your mother is fierce in protecting her young and she has made it clear to all that your Kelsey is hers." Father Fenn says with a whimsical smile.

"Mother, is so wild and you are so disciplined…" I ask. "How do you keep your sanity?"

My fathers both laugh. Father Fenn says, "It took time for her to beat our heads together enough to realize that we need to just love and trust her. She knows the boundaries and has never passed them, but she will do what she feels is the right thing to do." Father Fade nods his head. Tan is so much like Fade who doesn't talk much. Fenn continued, "Your Kelsey was very disciplined at the Council meeting. I could feel her frustration at the slow-witted behavior of some council members, but she stayed poised throughout" My chest puffed up at the words of my father.

She really was very well behaved at the meeting. Tan is surprised at the reminder of what transpired at the meeting.

"My mate is not usually so controlled." I admit, "I am grateful that she didn't go after the H'Atari council member. I was surprised to see a female representative from H'Atar."

"Yes, well, H'Atar has seemed to have a dearth of males lately, since the Galactic Federation forces took out all the An Ratha males at Gearin's wedding celebration. Most of the males have just disappeared." My father seems to be insinuating that the An Ratha's were more than just a crime family on H'Atar.

"I had heard there have been some attempts at mixing H'Atari with other races." Tan states, "Don Gaerin showed us that they had been successful in creating a mixed breed. Of course, it required genetic manipulation for success. Well, for the males. Our sources say Non-H'Atari females tend to die in labor. Probably why they are very quiet about their attempts."

This surprised me, *I never heard this. Where did you hear this?*

I read the briefings that were sent by the Intel Corp, Tan responded matter-of-factly. *Didn't you read them?*

I felt guilty, as I was used to Tan telling me the important details… Not the best practice, I am learning. *I must of missed that briefing.*

What is it our mate says? OK, Buddy, I believe you. Tan winks at me. He caught me.

Suddenly, all of us look at each other, Tan and I feel a sharp tremor of fear in our bond with Kelsey. ,

Ah, fuck. Not again. Then darkness. Our fathers are looking at us.

"Your mother and mate are in danger. A riot has broken out in the Shopping District," Father Fade states. "She says they have been separated from the guards and your mate has fainted."

Tet and I look at each other. "That isn't usual for our mate and her last thought suggests she didn't just faint," I explain as we run out of our quarters with our fathers right behind us.

"Teyana says she is being jostled about and has tried to keep a hold of Kelsey, but it is getting harder," Father Fenn yells as we run down the halls.

"Where are the City guards?" I am frantic because neither of us can feel our mate through the bond.

Will we ever be able to let her out of our sight again? Tan asks me.

We have to get her back safely first, I respond and send.

Hold on, my heart. We will find you, I send out into the darkness of the bond.

Chapter Twenty-Seven – Kelsey

The City within the space station fascinated me, and Teyana was so much fun to go out shopping with. However, I really wished to do more than all this "spend our males' money stuff.". I am not a kept woman. I have skills and the guys mentioned that I could work in Navigation when we are on the ship. Come on, I was studying astrophysics when I was abducted. I can read star charts. Shopping and going to lunch is not a great use of my big brain... well, my intelligence.

To be fair, my mother-in-law...or whatever Teyana is called on this side of the Galaxy...Is amazing. Plus, she did mention that she is only able to do this because she is on vacation from her job as a xenobiology researcher.

"So, we need to discuss my sons," Teyana suddenly says.

"Ohhhkayyyy?" That is so blunt; I have nothing better to respond with. What can I say to the mother of the males who want to claim me? "What can I say?" That is another brilliant line. I am not showing much in the way of my intelligence.

"I know that they are just like their fathers," She starts with. "What is the phrase you say, 'they have clubs up their anus'."

"Um. Sticks up their butts." I correct. Her way was just wrong.

"Oh yes, that is better. Cruder. I like it." She smiles impishly. "It is hard for them to move away from the discipline they learned from their fathers and then the military. Goddess knows, I tried to inject some fun into their lives, but sons like to emulate their fathers." She gives me a knowing look and I nod like I completely understand, though I don't know… "My two daughters are so much easier, both are in the science corps and will be thrilled to discuss mating between humans and other species with you and your friends. They know how to have a fun time."

"Are they twins?" I ask.

"Oh, no, on our planet, twins are always boys. I have only been pregnant five times. Three sets of boys." She smiles proudly. I am a bit shocked. "We are lucky we had those two females. Most families just have boys. But we have six boys and two girls. Tet and Tan are the oldest and most like their fathers. Jin and Jac have just started military training, so they are still a little under my influence. We are a small family by some standards, but we are not H'Atari who have twelve in a clutch. Females have three to six clutches in their lifetimes."

I am a bit stunned. "Wow! While humans have been known to have up to twenty kids. We usually only have two to three. Only the religious folk who don't believe in birth control have more than three or four. We just can't afford more than that due to a variety of issues. Folks no longer need large families to work the farms. Most jobs are being automated and, well, our planet can't handle the almost nine billion people we have now."

"There are nine billion humans?" Teyana is in shock now.

"Well, eight-point-seven or eight, but yeah, we have a lot of humans."

She shakes her head in disbelief. "We are lucky if we have thirty million on our whole planet and most species in the Galactic Federation have far less. Of course, we did at one time have billions throughout federated space, but that was during the wars and before disease swept the galaxy reducing the population by two thirds, almost two hundred years ago. I remember my grandmothers discussing those times. We were lucky that many of our most brilliant minds survived, but it devastated many worlds equally and did something to the genetics of many species. Females are rare. Fertile females are even rarer." She paused in reflection. "Some say that certain beings caused the disease as a means to eradicate their enemies but those species were not able to control it and caused their own species to either die out or begin to have the same issues."

"I seem to remember reading in my history classes about humans doing similar things during wars," I state. "They used chemicals that caused the soldiers fertility issues or caused cancer in their younglings, dying painful deaths. Killing a generation with their hate." I feel saddened that universally there are those that kill without thought of the consequences. "They killed for stupid reasons, because someone was different; different beliefs, different ethnicities, different sexuality and gender norms..." I just shake my head at the futility of it all.

"Well, we now know better," Teyana confirms, "but that does no stop those who are greedy from trying to wreak havoc in the Federation. Yet those criminals may have actually done some good. Eight billion people and you humans can breed with some of the species in the Federation."

"Well, don't encourage more abductions please," I plead.

"That, my dear, would be unethical." She smiles at me. "But I would like to see how well a mating with you and my sons go. I look forward to grandyounglings to spoil."

"It is that for life, thing that scares me." I confess.

"Why?" Teyana asks. "Are you afraid of being pleasured by males who only want the best for you?"

"I am afraid of being made to conform," I say. "I didn't do it for my family, why would I do it for a man…well, two males."

"My dear," she tucks my arm in hers, "No one is saying you have to conform. Do you think I conformed to my mates' ideas of a perfect obedient female?" Teyana snorts.

"Well, no, but…" I stammer.

"There are no buts. I made my mates dance a merry little dance before I settled down. They know that if they wanted me to confess my need for them that they needed to accept me for who I am. I am not a well-behaved female and neither was their mother." She winked at me with a bit of a smirk. "The males of this line love contrary women no matter what they say to the opposite. Just remember where you are when you decide to remind them that you are not as tame as they would like you to be. I heard that you were a perfect mate at the Council Meeting. Not one act of rebellion. My mates were very impressed by you. They will mention this to my sons who may…just may understand that your rebellion is for them and no one else."

"My mother would have been horrified if I didn't act professionally in a government forum." I am puffed up a bit by the fact that my mates' fathers were "impressed". "I was raised properly. Even if I chafe at the stupid things people expect of me."

"I understand this," Teyana agrees. "I hate Council meetings, but still need to be the perfect mate for my mates. This is why I just do not go." We start giggling at our own unsaid pact.

"I had to be there this time and anytime they are discussing humans." I smile like maybe this will work out.

I am glad you think so, my heart, Tet states smugly in my head.

Go away! I am not talking to you right now, I think back, my scowl obvious.

"So, my boys have a fairly strong link to you?" Teyana smiles. "Think how lovely it will be when you can wreak havoc with them from afar."

"You can do that?" I ask.

" Oh, yes, yes I can," She smirks. "Fenn and Fade have had to learn to keep still while I play with them during meetings."

"I thought you could shut off the link?" I am intrigued.

"Yes and no." Her eyes wink merrily. "After you are claimed, they will still feel your emotions even if you block your thoughts. So if you were to …say…pleasure yourself during one of their dull meetings…"

"OMG!!! That sounds like fun!" I squeal, "though don't tell me anymore, because that may just be too much information from the mother of my mates." OK, fucking with their meetings sounds like a great reason to let them claim me. Not really, but I do like that pair of sticks in the mud.

I am not a stick in the mud. Tan huffs.

I thought I blocked you two.

You blocked Tet, but I can still hear your thoughts, Tan sends an air of smugness. That is when I block him. *I really have to get better at blocking.*

Teyana continue our conversation as we walk through the promenade of the city. Our guards seem a bit uneasy with the crowds of people that are filling the streets. We continue down, but they stop us and look at Teyana. The large Minotaur-looking dude speaks.

"Lady Teyana, I would suggest we head back to your quarters. The crowd is not looking too friendly." Just as he says that, a fight starts up ahead of us and quickly turns into a melee. As the fight grows, the guards are being jostled around while Teyana and I try to quickly move between them. Before I get a chance to move into the protective circle of our guards, I feel a familiar prick on my neck. I see Teyana grabbing me as I go down.

"Ah, fuck. Not again." And the world goes black.

Chapter Twenty-Eight – Ab'Nel

My Lord, we got one!" The excited minion states over the com. I like that I am now referred to as a "Lord". As head of the An Ratha Family it is only appropriate, but, right now, I am feeling the weight of this responsibility.

"What do you mean, you have one?" I was worried about what I was going to hear next. He is lucky we are on a long distance com or he would see my frown at his bothering me.

"We recaptured one of the females! We got intel that she was going to be in the shopping district with the mate of the former Akkadian Council, Lady Teyana." He sounds so smug, the cretin.

"You mean the mate of the Akkadian Command Team of *The Patience?*" I growl out.

"Nah, boss. She does not have the mating bite." He is clueless, and he just kept talking… "She was just wandering around with the lady and her guards. It was great! We had Bhud punch a Gontoran and it started an amazing riot. It allowed B'kee to sneak in tranq her. It was flawless!... Well, almost." He pauses.

"M'Quu, what happened?" My fingers pinch my nose ridge as a headache threatens.

"Well, my Lord." He hesitates. "She just would not let go of the human and we tried to pull her off." My brain hurts, this is bad really bad.

"M'Quu, I am afraid to ask, but WHAT. DID. YOU. DO?"

"Do not worry, boss. We will take care of the old female!"

"WHAT.. DID.. YOU.. DO?" I repeat.

"We will find a way to extract her and leave her somewhere for the night guard to find. But she just keeps clinging to the human. Who knew an old female would be so strong. We can not extract her!" I can hear a note in the idiot's voice that he is starting to understand the trouble he is causing me.

"First off, who told you to capture the human?" I inquire.

"Cap'n Schnel'Dn's last orders were to find and capture all the females." He is obtuse.

"Is Schnel'Dn in charge?" I ask, waiting for the obvious answer.

"Well… no…He's …dead. But those were his last orders!" Still not quite getting it.

"Yes, he is dead, because of his stupidity," I yell. "And do you know what you have done?"

"I …I …I followed orders and retrieved one of the females, my lord." I sigh at his stupidity.

"Please say you did not take the females on board our ship." I am going to settle this.

"No sir. The Council Guard have swarmed the station and we have not been able to transport the females beyond the safe house." Thank the Universe for small mercies.

"Stay there. We will have someone come and take charge of the females. Out!" I know what needs to be done as I cut the com.

"What is the matter, my love?" My mate stands in the doorway. Her arms are crossed over her chest showing that she heard the conversation and is making plans to mitigate the issue. Her stomach shows our successful breeding. I smile at her. She will lay the eggs soon then brood with the help of the H'Atari Genetic team we have hired. I will not have problems with my offspring and my mate will know that I am on top of the situation without her interference.

"We just need to do some new hiring," I tell her, "It seems some of our men made the mistake of thinking that an Akkadian mating is all about the claim and not just the sex." Her eyes narrow as I grab my com and say the code.

"Yes, My Lord?" The deep voice on the other side states.

"I am terminating the employment of M'Quu and his gang. They are at the safe house," I state. "Let the Akkadians take care of the females then clean up afterwards."

"Yes, Sir." I smile, knowing the Shu'Bak will do his job well. Grabbing my mate and taking her to the bedroom. I am going to enjoy fucking this ugly female knowing that I have all I have wanted and no more mistakes will be allowed.

Chapter Twenty-Nine - Kelsey

I wake feeling like I am in a vice. What the hell is going on? Then I try to look behind me. In my periphery I see Teyana's white hair and a flash of black skin.

"Teyana?" I ask in a half-whisper.

"Oh good, you are awake." She loosens her arms, allowing me to turn and sit up. We are sitting on a cot in a small, plain room. "I could not let go of you. You were out and they would have stolen you away." She gives me a hug before continuing. "I have contacted my mates and they are on their way. To where? I do not know. Those criminals threw a bag over my head. Oh, they are not going to be happy when my mates and sons get here."

I look around the room and see it doesn't have a window, just a door.

One way in, one way out, I think.

Kelsey, my heart? You're awake! I hear Tet and Tan in my head.

Yeah, I just woke up. Your mother is here... Wherever here is..

We know, our fathers have been in contact with her, Tan sends me. *We will be there soon. Just do not let the criminals know. We want to surprise them.*

Of course you do. I am still nervous of what can happen. *Be careful. I need my mates.* I mean it. I need them right now and forever. I may not know how I will deal with their stiff personalities, but I can't live without them.

Nor can we live without you, Tet reminds me they are able to hear my thoughts.

Shush, go away! I tell him.

Does this mean, we can claim you after we find you?. Tan asks.

I didn't say that. But the thought made me happy.

You did not have to, my love, we feel your answer. Tet feels positively smug at that.

"My mates say they are almost here, but we need…"

"…To act scared," I finish for her. "Tet and Tan say the same thing. I am beginning to think there is an advantage to this telepathy thing."

"There is. However, it is very limited until you are fully claimed," Teyana says. "If they get us out of this, you should work on that, my dear." I smile at her.

"So, we are still on the Council Station?" I ask.

"Yes, at least, I am pretty sure as I did not hear any sounds that indicated we were on a ship." Teyana confirmed. Suddenly, there are some noises outside of the door.

"The boss is angry! We are dead." I hear a rough voice. "We need to get those females out of here and see if we can sell them on the market."

"But the old female is mated to high up Akkadianans!" Another gravely voice croaks.

"Did you not hear me? 'His lordship' is pissed!" the first one says. "We need to get off this station. But you are correct. Kill the old one. It might make the boss happy if those righteous bastards die with the elimination of their mate!" We hear the males stomping to the door.

I hug Teyana tightly to me. She is holding me just as tightly. We have no problem pretending to be scared because we are scared…really scared.

As the door starts to slide open, we hear the crash at the front of the hideout. The door closes again and there is a lot of shouting, roars, bumps and bangs. The hat door opened and a greasy, dark haired alien scooted in before closing it again. He held a gun like weapon towards Teyana and I.

"Tell them to back off or I kill you both," he says.

"Well, that won't help you at all will it," I say flippantly. "Kill us, you're dead. Keep us alive, you can be protected with the right information."

"What do you mean?" He is rightly suspicious. The door must be locked because I can hear banging on the door and feel my mates on the other side.

"Well, if you tell us who your 'boss' is we can negotiate some safety for you."

My heart, we can not promise anything to that fiend, Tet says in my mind.

It is a chance to find the masterminds, right? I return. I keep my eyes on the ugly man.

"He will kill me," the Midagian whimpers.

"Aren't you dead already?" I ask, hoping life is like the TV shows I enjoyed. "At least, with the Galactic Federation officers, you have a chance."

"Well, maybe." He hedges.

"Show our mates that you are valuable and I am sure they will protect you." I bat my eyes and look innocent. "Like, where is your boss now?"

"I do not know." Looking at me with more hesitancy: "it is bigger than him and that creature he is mated to."

"He is mated?" I ask, realizing this guy isn't the sharpest crayon in the box.

"Yeah, he mated the head of the An Ratha Family. A real ugly female." Suddenly, the air shimmered, a large dark figure appeared - *pfpht, pew pew* - and the figure disappeared in a shimmer as the Misagian fell dead at our feet. Teyana and I looked at our feet. I was in shock as Teyana rushed to the door letting our mates enter the room. He was telling us the information we needed, but he is dead. I have never had anyone die in front of me. I wish I could be as great as Teyana, but I am frozen. The guy is dead. Killed in…front…of me. I try to justify this situation. This guy is a bad man, why am I freaking? Tet and Tan surround me and take me in their arms. I don't feel the tears in my eyes, but I know that I am crying. I am in shock. This shit is so real.

It is all going to be fine, my heart. Tet says to me.

He is dead. I was talking to him and he is dead. I am trying to make sense of the scene in front of me. Teyana's mates turn the male over. There is a hole in the corpse's body, where a heart should be, all blackened like it was cauterized, as there isn't any blood. His eyes are opened wide in surprise, yet vacant of life. I can't take this and bury my head into Tan's chest. His hand is on the back of my head. His chin on the top. Murmuring soothing words to me in his roughened voice.

"It is hard the first time you face death, my heart," Tan tells me. Tet is pressed against my back.

Cry it out, if you need, Tet sends. *We are here. You are safe and he is no longer in the pain of this existence.*

He was telling me the information we needed and he was killed right here…in front of me. I look up at Tan then back to Tet. I look at their parents, Teyana being hugged by their fathers.

"It looks like a Shu'Bak disruptor," Fade stated. Teyana looks at me with a concerned look.

"My dear, the assassin used transport tech that is still new. He probably was listening in to the conversation," she states. "He was probably here to 'clean up' the mess made by this Misagian."

"The 'Boss' must be well read or fairly good at intelligence collection," Fenn states. "He probably knows that we would not be too far behind these thugs and ordered the hit."

"Let's head home; the Council Guards will be here to clean up this place." Tet instructs. I start to get up off the cot when I am swung up into Tet's arms and he strides to the door.

"I can walk, you know!" I am a little miffed that he thinks I am incapacitated.

I know you can, my heart. But I need to hold you for my sanity. Ah, that is so sweet. *The sooner I claim you the better it will be for me.* I thump his chest at that.

"You think after this trauma I am ready to be claimed?" I say with indignation.

"My dear, do not tease the boys," Teyana lightly scolds me. "Anyone can see they are desperate for you. Besides, if they claim you, you will not have to worry about situations like this."

"Teyana, you and I know that being claimed for safety is not a great relationship starter," I scold back.

"Yes, dear, but it will be very fun to be claimed by two handsome Akkadianans like my sons. So much fun." She smirks rubbing her hands up her mates arms, as my mouth opens in shock at that. "Close your mouth dear, you do not want to catch dlyxs." I snap my mouth shut then and allow my mates to take me home.

Chapter Thirty - Tan

I march right into our quarters with our mate in our arms. I am done playing her games. She will let us claim her or else…I do not know what.

I cannot stand the thought of you coming to harm, my heart. I look down into her face with all the love I have for this beautiful human. *You must let us complete the claiming. You are too precious*!

"Tan, listen to me." She looks at me and I feel the pain in her lovely eyes. "I want you… both of you … to claim me, but now, it isn't the right time. I want it to be special because you claiming me should be special, not just a trauma response." Her hands palm my face.

Our mate is wise, brother. Tet walks in the room. *I, too, am fearful from almost losing our mate, but she is right we must wait to claim her. She is too special for the claiming to be done because we are scared.*

"Thank you!" our mate says. "Marriage…mating is a lifelong commitment and should be done with all proper respect." *Wow, I can't believe that came out of my mouth,* Kelsey thinks. A smile forms on my lips.

It did, my heart, I let her know.

"Shit, I forgot to block you two." She sighs. " I need to just relax tonight, OK?"

She wraps her arms around me in a hug that asks only for comfort. I respond in kind and pull her in my arms more firmly, kissing the top of her head. I guide her to the big lounger in the room that wraps around. Tet joins us as we just sit holding each other. His arms stretch around her from the opposite side, allowing us to just sit there and comfort her. Tet and I take turns over the afternoon smoothing our hands through her golden strands. Her head moves from one shoulder to the other, her breathing steady, but not so relaxed that she sleeps. We just sit there, calmly enjoying the feel of our mate between us. She is safe and in our arms. At this moment, we can't ask for much more.

Unfortunately, our time of peace is shattered by the shrill tone of Tet's com. He looks at it and responds, "We are on our way….Yes, we will bring our mate. We are not willing to leave her alone or with guards right now. See you in 30," He touches the com and turns to us.

"They want to debrief us on the abduction. The higher ups are concerned that these criminals are staging riots in the Shopping District in order to capture their targets."

"I was enjoying our quiet time," Kelsey said.

I was too, my heart, I tell her. Surprisingly, I miss just holding her peacefully. Just sitting there with our mate sandwiched between Tet and I. Since meeting Kelsey, I have never felt this calm.

We better head out. Tet reminds us. I reluctantly release my mate and stand next to Tet with my hand out to her. I am relieved when she takes it and I have that connection that I need to remain calm around this beautiful creature that is our mate.

▪▪

We sit at the far end of the Council boardroom, as the Senior Council goes over Kelsey and Mother's testimony.

"We still do not know who the new head of the An Ratha family is." Senior Council Ar'Arith addresses everyone. "However, we know they are possibly mated to a Misagian Captain. One who is connected to the abductions of humans."

"That is what the male said, sir," My mate is doing well in front of the five council members.

"A criminal!" Councilor Tri'Acrera yells. "You trust the word of a criminal. The An Ratha family are just a group of respectable females. They could not help that their males were causing so many problems that we had to call in the Marines of the Galactic forces. And to even consider females, it is unthinkable."

"Ma'am, respectfully. That criminal was murdered while telling me this information," Kelsey speaks up. "And you know that females are just as competent as males. You, yourself, are a female in a male dominated field. Are you saying you can't lead?"

Her thin lipped mouth gaped at me. I blinked my eyes at her. "By the way, on Earth, some of our greatest criminals were females. They tended to terrorize their regions for years and no one suspected that a lady would be that ruthless. What better way to hide a criminal enterprise and if one of them has allied with essentially a pirate enterprise, you should realize that this could make your job harder."

"How so?" The counselor is intrigued.

"Well, I assume you are an honorable politician. Who has to maintain a high level of integrity in your dealings." *I see what you are doing, my heart.* I smile proudly at her. *Shush you, I am working here.* This is my mate. "If people think you are in league with this criminal enterprise you may lose credibility. Besides, you wouldn't want them to think you can't handle your job because you are just a lowly female. Now, would you?"

"Females are just as competent as males," Tri'Acrera confirmed. "I am not so sure that one of our prominent families is involved, but I will keep my eyes on the females that our leading the family. My cousin married into the family. It was considered a good match for him. Though they made him change his name and he was one of the males who died at that ceremony."

"Yes, the mating ceremony," Commander Max is speaking now. "Where all the An Ratha males were there to witness the forced mating of Don Gaerin An Ratha to Admiral D'Artemus's mate, Elizabeth."

"Another human," the H'Atari counselor states. She looks at Kelsey and asks, "What is it with you humans that our males are going crazy for you?"

Be careful, my heart. We do not want to make her more of an enemy, I warn Kelsey.

Have a little faith in me, she tells me. "Your Honor, I don't know why the Universe has brought these males to me. Lord knows Earth women seem to have as hard a time as your females do finding good males to marry…uh…mate with. Maybe you need to work with other females to find good males. Don't you have a friend you can trust to tell you if a guy is nice or a real creep. Of course, males should take baths and work to please you." The Misagian council member looks uncomfortable. "If you really can lay clutches of babies, then that is a great opportunity for any males who are compatible with your race. I think we are attractive to males who are compatible with humans. We carry our young for nine months and generally only have one baby at a time. Though we can carry twins and triplets, but that isn't the usual." The councilmember from H'Atari seems to be thoughtful. *Well, I can't very well tell her she looks like a bug, poor thing.*

I maintain a straight face, but Tet and I really need to get our mate home. She is too smart and was going to cause us to lose it here in front of the councilmembers assembled.

Tet stands up, "Councilmembers, please excuse us. Our mate is tired and needs to go back to our quarters to rest. She has had quite the day and was witness to the murder of our only witness."

We lead our mate to the door, but as we enter the corridor, the Senior Council waylays us. "Before you go. May I meet with you in your quarters? I have some thing of a delicate matter to discuss with your mate." I look at Tet and we give a nod.

"Good…good. I will be there in 45?" he says hesitantly.

I wonder why he wants the privacy of our quarters? I say as we walk down the hall, away from the Senior Council as he returns to the boardroom.

"Oh, I think I know," Kelsey says. "I wonder if he will bring her with him. I really would like to see Yaretzi." With that, we return to our quarters.

Chapter Thirty-One – Kelsey

I walk into our quarters and head to the couch. "Come here, you two. I want to cuddle, before our guests come." I tell my mates.

You want to what? Tan asks me through the bond.

"Cuddle," I roll my eyes at them, "You know just holding each other for comfort, not sex."

We do not know this cuddle, but for you, my heart, we will do what you ask. Tet wraps himself on my right, while Tan is on my left.

"You have never cuddled before or after sex?" I ask.

No, my heart, before you, sex was just an act with strangers and not many of those. Tan states as he wraps his arms around me and squeezes gently.

All memories of others disappeared when we first met you. Tet emphasizes his statement with a squeeze from the opposite side from Tan.

"I will say, you two take good care of me in the bedroom," I smirk. "For that I am thankful for those nameless females. I have never felt as I do with you."

While I am glad that we please you, I would prefer you forget those other males. Tan is a little tense and growly.

"Don't worry, Tan." I rub his chest over his heart. and give him a sly smile. "I forgot those others when your magic tongue pulled orgasm after orgasm from me."

Just wait for when we claim you, you will never be satisfied by any but us. Tet chimes in.

"Somehow, I think it will be more than the sex, my love." I gently kiss Tet's lips, then I move to kiss Tan. Both try to move closer. Their hands sliding along my sides and petting my shoulders, neck and along my chin. Who knows where we would be if the chime on the door didn't sound right at that moment.

My mates jump from the couch. Tet calls out "Enter". The door opens to reveal the Senior Council and Yaretzi.

"Hey, buddy!" I call to her as I stand to greet her. "How is this stuffed shirt treating you?" She laughs and moves to hug me.

"Will you tell this dick to leave me alone?" she whispers to me.

"Is he hurting you? I will kick his ass!" I tell her.

"No, no, he just keeps saying I am his mate and that his tattoo proves it." Yaretzi is frantic.

"Well, it kind of is the way around here," I tell her. "Tet…Tan, pull up your sleeves." Showing their matching mating marks. "See…Oh wow, they have grown." My mates grin mischievously.

"Of course, we are closer in our bond. It will grow larger when we take you fully," Tet states with one of those sexy smirks.

"And you, Senior Council, have these mating marks?" I ask of the big man.

"Of course, I would have nothing to do with this troublesome female, if not for the marks that say she is my fated one." He shows the marks that radiate from his wrists halfway up his fore arm. He is really grumpy.

"Well, if I were you, I would think about an attitude adjustment," I say to the big male who is my mates' boss. "As my Mom says, 'you catch more flies with honey', I look at Yaretzi. "Is he trying to boss you around."

"*Dios mio*, YES!" she rolls her eyes to emphasize her frustration. However, I notice something in her eyes as she looks at him…Hmmmm.

"Come with me," I drag her into the bedroom, with a backward thought. *No listening in, boys! Girl talk. You entertain Chuckles there.*

Who is Chuckles? Tan asks

Figure it out! as I block them.

Closing the door, I turn to Yaretzi and walk to the big bed sitting down and patting the bed beside me. She sits next to me, her fingers picking on the beautiful skirt she wears.

"You look good." I decide to start with a little small talk.

"R'Alas had his aide help me get 'appropriate clothes," She smooths the silky fabric.

"It is a beautiful outfit," I say to her.

"Yeah, Qn'Cil has great taste." She looks a little guilty.

"So, the Senior Council is being brutish and trying to force you into something you don't want?" I ask.

"Oh, no. He hasn't even touched me," She is quick to say. "He says that I will beg for him to claim him."

"Sounds like a cocky asshole, huh? Are you even slightly attracted to him?" A sly smile comes on her face.

"Oh, yeah, I am very attracted to the *pendejo*. But he is so bossy and keeps telling me what to do and how I should act, like I am a little doll." She looks up and sighs. "I just don't think I should change for anyone. Is that so wrong."

"Oh, no, not at all," I assure her. "So, he is trying to get you to be the proper mate of a councilmember."

"Exactly!" she grabs my hands, "you understand."

"Of course, you have seen the clowns I am with?" I chuckle.

What are clowns, my heart. I am thinking you are not giving a favorable impression of us. Tan says through the bond.

Didn't I tell you not to eavesdrop? I respond to him. *This girl needs to know that bossiness is just a cultural thing.* And then I blocked him.

"Have you tried to kiss him?" I ask.

"What! I am not going to kiss that man…male!" She blushes.

"But you want to, don't you?" I think this woman is smitten but is dealing with some of the same stuff I went through.

She sighs. "Yes, yes I want to and more. I mean, have you looked at him. He is HOT."

I giggle. "Well, my two are extremely attractive. I am not really into the turquoise boys."

"You know, I am a virgin." She gives me a serious look.

"What? You're kidding, right?" I am in shock right now.

"I just never found a guy I wanted to give it up to." She shrugs her shoulders. "I mean, I have…you know…for myself, but I just didn't go there with a guy."

"Oh, OK, so we need to get this male to see your worth."

"What? No! There is no worth in being a virgin at my age. I am not Victoria!" We both giggle at our friend's purity culture attitudes.

"So, what do you want?" I ask.

"I want him to see me," she whispers. "Not just be a biological urge. I need to be loved. Am I crazy? To expect this. I know your Captain mentioned that we women would need mates, but why this guy for me."

"I don't know why, but Tet and Tan have changed much of their attitude for me," I say to her. "I guess, we have gotten to know each other and, well, I love them."

We love you too, Both of my mates respond.

"Don't make me come out there and hit you two assholes!" I scream. "I may love you, but you will see what happens when you piss me off!"

Sorry for intruding, my heart, Tet responds. *If it makes you feel better, we are explaining to the Senior Council that he might want to take a gentler track with your friend.*

Yeah, well. You had a learning curve too. I have a smirk on my face.

"So, you have a telepathic link with your guys." She looks at me.

"Yep. It makes private conversations a bit of a problem." Then I smile wickedly. "Their mother gave me ways to get back at them." I start thinking of what I would do to the pair of them when our guests leave… Oh, yeah…I feel them both responding to those naughty thoughts of mine

My heart, you are an evil female! We are with the Senior Council. This is so inappropriate. Tan is pleading with me.

I feel Tet's humor at the situation. *Just wait until we get you alone, my heart. You will feel the consequences of your thoughts.*

Sounds like a promise. I think sassily.

It is, my heart, it most definitely is. I feel Tet block me as he turns his attention to our esteemed guest.

I tell Yaretzi to stay strong and make sure her male figures out that she isn't some passive female. I just hope she is able to bring that male to her way of thinking. I think she will be happy with the big lug if he just stops with all the stuffy idiocy that seems to be more common with these guys. I know that I have my mates where I want them.

After a while, the Senior Council and my friend said their goodbyes and left us for our evening. I think I am feeling a lot better after my adventures, but I just want to head to bed after some dinner or so my stomach tells me…loudly.

Come, my heart. Tan gets my attention. *We need to feed you. I can hear your stomach growling.*

You shouldn't mention that, I tell him. *It isn't polite to mention body noises to a lady.*

Tan smirks. *And you are a lady. My lady...my mate.* His mate, I like that. Despite all my bluster and handwringing. I really do love these guys. Not just in love, but I love them. I have never felt like this before. My mates lead me to the table and, sitting on each side of me, start to feed me bits and pieces of the food on the table in the dining area of the living space.

"I think I can feed myself, gentlemen." I tell them in between bites of the delicious food.

"It is our duty to feed our precious mate, my heart," Tet replies.

Tan leans forward and starts nibbling on my neck. *Hmmm, that feels good.* I really need to stop him but ohhhh that feels lovely. "Tan, my love. Please." I mumble. "Not now, please let me have the time I asked for."

He sits up and gives a hot and hungry look that belies the, *Yes, my heart.* he sends me. We finish our dinner in a soft quiet. I am so tired and my eyes are heavy. Tet gently lifts from the chair and carries me to our bedroom. The two of them work together to undress me and put me into the center of the bed and I fall asleep as they slip under the covers with me.

Chapter Thirty-Two – Tet

I wake up to my mate stabbing me in the stomach with her knee as she tries to climb over. "Oooomph!" comes out of my mouth involuntarily.

"Sorry, Tet." She finishes her slide over me. "I gotta go."

"Go where?" I say with concern.

"To put it indelicately…I gotta go pee…now." She runs for the sanitary room.

Our mate is adorable in the morning, Tan says to me.

I rub my stomach, still a bit sore from that pointy little knee. *Oh yes, she is, but she needs to climb out on your side of the bed.*

Tan chuckles at my misfortune. I give him a backhanded punch to the gut.

She is ours…she is really ours to keep… and breed. Tan has an aura of wonder with that thought. I nod. We haven't claimed her yet, but we will when the time is right. I hope it is soon.

The door to the sanitary room opens up and Kelsey sticks her head out. "I am going to make use of this huge shower. Anyone want to join me and see if we can use all the hot water?" Tan and I are racing to the door. Kelsey giggles as we are in the shower with her within seconds.

Tan grabs the washcloth and soaps it up while I turn Kelsey towards me with her back to him. He begins rubbing the cloth over her back as I kiss her lips, as I move my hands over her body. Tan lifts her right arm, rubbing the cloth under that arm. He then lifts the left arm and cleans that side. I nibble at her lower lip, my hands enjoying the weight of her breasts. I nibble down her chin then her neck, reveling in the taste of her. Tan hands me the soapy cloth and I meticulously begin cleaning her front.

Kelsey takes the cloth from me and rubs over my chest and down my stomach. I inhale deeply as her hand wraps around my very core. My cock was awake but now, it is so stiff it hurts. I groan as that tiny hand moves up and down the length. She moves a bit sideways and I feel Tan in her grip. She has us both in her hands, as she kneels down on the floor of the shower. The cloth drops to the floor beside her.

Oh, my heart, you are magical! Tan's eyes are closed as he enjoys the feel of our mate. Kelsey has turned towards me and her tongue licks the bulbous head of my cock as she continues to stroke Tan.

Gods, that feels so good, Kelsey has taken my flesh into her mouth. I look down at her beautiful head to see those plump lips circling my turgid cock. One hand moves to the top of her head, while the other reaches back to the shower wall. I am overcome with the feeling of that sweet, sweet mouth sucking my very essence from me. She pulls off of me and turns to Tan, gifting him with her lips.

By all that is holy, my heart! he groans. Kelsey doesn't neglect me as she licks and suckles Tan. No, she continues to pump me with her hand.

"Come, my heart. We need you now!" I cry as I feel my balls grow heavy. I pull her off the ground and turn off the shower. "We are clean enough." Tan moans in a mild protest as her lips are detached from his engorged penis. I grab a towel and dry my mate off and begin moving her to the bed. Tan is right behind us. Like me, he barely dries as he moves quickly to grab our mate. We work together to lay her on the bed and spread those gorgeous legs baring her sex to us. *Paradise!* We think together. All that flowering pinkness is before us. I elbow him as I dive in to take a taste of our mate.

She is already wet for us. My tongue swipes between her legs making her moan. I grab her legs and wrap them over my shoulders. Tan punches my shoulder, before diving for her breasts. Now, our mate is wiggling under our ministrations. I feel her pleasure. She is mindless with the power of our tongues sucking and licking her clit and breasts.

"Oh God…Oh Tet…Yeah, right there…Oh Tan," She is whimpering, moaning then screaming. "Fuck me! Fuck me NOW!" Her cream is pouring from her core. My tongue is up into that passage drinking more of that sweetness. Nothing is better than her cum. When I am satisfied that she is ready, I look at Tan and he nods.

"My heart, are you ready to be claimed?" We ask. I out loud and Tan in his manner. She looks at each of us. She nods.

"Yes, I am a bit scared, but yes, please claim me." That is all we need. Tan and I pull up onto our knees sandwiching her between us. Tan is on her front and I have her lovely back to me when we lift her.

Spread your legs, my heart, Tan orders her, as I move in. My cock is hard and throbbing between Kelsey's butt cheeks. I bend over her back, my arms wrapping around her and my hands cupping her magnificent breasts. Slowly, I line my penis up to her core and enter that tunnel. My cock is so ready and so hard, I have a hard time keeping from releasing. Once I am settled, I pull her back, and open her for Tan. He moves quickly into position and lines up his throbbing cock pushing in next to mine.

We move in and out in sync, one at a time filling Kelsey with both of our shafts. She moans incoherently, but we feel her rapture as we drive into that tight cunt, made all the tighter with both of us. I can feel her passion rising even higher as we take that delightful hole. My brother and I are almost ready to blow, the feeling is just too powerful. Both of us take a side of Kelsey's neck, nibbling and kissing along the sides up from her collar and down from her neck. "Please, please, please." She is moaning. The sound of her uncontrolled voice is causing Tan and I to speed up as we start to lose control. As she screams out her orgasm, her muscles tighten around us. Tan and I lose control and begin pumping harder and faster. I can feel our balls tightening and enlarging as we become animalistic with our primal need to fill Kelsey's womb. As our seed bursts out of our cocks her pussy milks them, both of our heads sway back as our canines extend. As if we are one, Tan and I bite down on our quivering mate's neck, injecting the mating venom into her as our cocks push our life force into her womb.

We are complete. I can feel everything about my mate. I see her past; her childhood, that fateful birthday that brought her to us. Her world and her life is part of us now. Tan's happiness is overwhelming, as tears stream from his eyes. Kelsey's eyes are wide as she realizes the whole effect of having been claimed.

"Whoa! It is like I have your memories?" she is questioning.

"Yes, my heart. Our souls are truly joined." I smile at her as she looks from Tan to me.

It is like they know everything. She tries to block us, causing me to smile.

Tan chuckles. *That, my hear, is because we do.*

Chapter Thirty-Three - Kelsey

You were such a cute and wicked little kid. I give him a smile then hauled off and hit Tan's arm, then Tet's. "So, my mind is completely open to you two?" I yell at them.

ı ɛs, my heart," Tet says hesitantly. I can feel their anxiety and concern.

Taking a deep breath, I take in their thoughts and feelings. "So, none of us can hide anything from each other?"

No, my heart. We cannot have secrets. Tan is starting to relax. *Though we may not be able to hear your thoughts at a great distance, we can feel your emotions and your state of mind.*

I try to work out my feelings. I don't have much of a choice. One thing about this claiming: I am very aware of my body, as well as their minds. This morning there is a spark of something low in my body. I am not sure, but it definitely feels like something is happening. I can feel cells splitting and attaching to me. Surely, I can't be... Noooo, that is not something that can be felt yet...Can it?

It is quite possible, my heart, Tet confirms. *The claiming bite can heighten certain senses and adjust hormones to enhance the chance of breeding.*

"But how can I be pregnant this fast, let alone feel it?" I question. Oh, that feeling of smug maleness rolled off the both of them. This was starting to boil my blood.

"You have a fever, my heart?" Tet asks. Rolling my eyes, I could only chuckle. They just don't understand.

No fever, you are upset? Tan asks next, I feel him as they both begin figuring it out. I am upset because they didn't warn me.

But we told you that there would be a much stronger connection between us. Tan is so sincere.

"Yes, but I guess I couldn't imagine how open my mind would be to you." I am still wrapping my head around all this.

"Is there a reason you would want to keep secrets from us?" Tet inquires and his white eyebrow raises like *Star Trek's* Spock. Oops, well, I guess I don't really need to keep secrets. "No, you do not!" Tet wraps his arms around me and nuzzles my ear. "You will always be with us mentally, even when you are physically away from us."

Wow! This is really weird, yet kind of cool even if I can't sneak out when I need to... *And, yes, I do need to sneak out every so often, you two busy bodies.* Tet and Tan give me a look that says it all. I don't think I will be sneaking out very often. But I will be safe.

Very safe, my heart. my mates respond. Then it hits me. I could be pregnant. OMG! Me ... a mom?

You will be the best mother, Tan assures me.

"I need your mother to come with me to see Michelle." I look at my mates with a worried gaze. "I need to know if it is true and I need to know what to expect."

"My beautiful agent of chaos needs to know what to expect?" Tet chuckles.

"Yeah, I do like to have a plan for important things and I would say THIS qualifies for an important thing." I like being spontaneous, but not about something so important. "Tet…Tan, I am scared." Both of my mates wrap their arms around me and cuddle me. This is so overwhelming but I guess I will just have to muddle through and trust that my mates will be there for me.

You know we will, Tan states.

Aaaannnndddd…That is another thing I will need to get used to, annoying busy bodies in my brain.

What is a busy body? Tet asks.

YOU! Listening in on my thoughts, I tell him.

I love you, my heart, he begins. *Your thoughts are important to us. Besides, I think your thoughts are adorable.*

Asshole, I state as he smiles. "I love you too. Now, I need to get an appointment with Michelle and see if your mom can come."

Chapter Thirty-Four – Kelsey

It took a few days to get into the medics office. In that time, my mates and I couldn't get enough of each other. I was still freaked out by the possibility of being a mom and, of course, now I didn't have any privacy. My mates are learning to not comment on every little thing I think. I can almost…almost…forget that they are able to hear every thought and emotion.

I am so happy to see Michelle. She stands next to that big male; I saw her with at the meeting. She gives me a big hug. Teyana stands next to me. I can feel her excitement.

"This is my Mother-in-law, Teyana Bl'wski. Tayana, this one of my friends, Michelle…" I flounder. Looking at Michelle in shock. "I'm sorry, I don't know your last name."

Michelle laughs. "I don't think it ever came up in conversation on the ship. It's Laurent. Michelle Genevieve Laurent. It is so nice to meet you, Lady Teyana."

"A pleasure to meet you, Lady Michelle," Teyana looks at me. "What is a mother-in-law?"

"Oh, I am sorry." I realize that I forgot the cultural differences again. "A mother-in-law is the mother of your spouse…um, your mates."

"Mother-in-law? Hmm, I like that." Teyana tries it on for size. She hugs me and declares, "I am your mother-in-law. You get to call me Mother!" She is more a mother to me than my own. My heart grew so big that I hugged her even harder.

"We should get you in the exam room and see where you are at," Michelle cuts in. "Is that meet with your approval, Senior Medic O'Jectic?" She glares at the big, purple alien.

"Yes, of course." His deep voice makes me look at Michelle with that look. "Lady Bl'wski, I am here to learn more about humans and hybrid pregnancies. This is the first Akkadianan/human hybrid we have seen. Our medics are still studying human anatomy though we have noticed many similarities."

"Well, it is good you have Michelle," I say. "She knows human anatomy."

His eyebrow lifts. "Yes, she knows human anatomy and we appreciate that. However, she will need to learn about the anatomy of eighteen new species." Michelle gives him a sour look.

"The anatomies are not THAT different," Michelle argues.

"How many hearts does a Miterian have?" the big guy asks her.

"Do we need to discuss this right now?" Michelle looks at him with impatience. "I have a *human* patient right now." She leads me to the examination table with him following her. The Senior Medic leans over her and whisper just loud enough for me to hear. "if there was an emergency right now, you know that Miterian would want you to know it's anatomy." Michelle hisses at him, as she sits me down and assists me to lay down on the table.

"They have a primary heart and an auxiliary one." He looks pleased with her answer.

"You have been studying, my mate." Michelle struggles to keep a smile off her face but I feel her pride at answering correctly. That is weird. I feel her emotions.

You will feel the emotions of others, my heart, Tan interrupts my thoughts. *It is what makes Akkadianans are such good diplomats and military leaders.*

Thank you for the information. Now shoo! I smile with exasperation.

Michelle has a wand in her hand and she waves it over my body from head to toes. I didn't need to undress. A hologram appears over me. There are four screens, one shows what I think is my nervous system. Another is my skeletal system. The third shows my muscles and, finally, there is a list I can't read. "Wow! That is a handy little scanner," I say. "What does this screen say," pointing to the writing on that one screen. Teyana answers me.

"They are growing well!" she sounds excited.

"They???" I question. "I can't be more than a few days pregnant if at all. How can you tell."

"A few days is common for Akkadianans to show pregnancy and the number of young you carry on a scanner," Teyana replies. "Why? How long does it take for humans?"

"Generally, six weeks to show on standard pregnancy tests," Michelle answers her. "Twelve to fourteen weeks to detect multiples. Generally, towards the end of the first trimester, beginning of the Second."

"How long are your pregnancies?" Teyana asks.

"Typically, nine months, give or take one of our lunar cycles," Michelle responds.

"Oh my." Teyana holds my hands, "Well, don't you worry, Kelsey. You will be happy to know that Akkadianan pregnancies last only five to six galactic months."

I am thrilled, as I remember Elizabeth saying she could carry up to fifteen months. But such a short pregnancy means I will blow up like a balloon quickly.

And we will be thrilled to see you carrying our sons, Tet lets me know he hears my side of the conversation.

Sons, I think. *How do you know…Oh wait, your mother told me only boys come in multiples.*

"If you are talking to my sons," Teyana says. "Let them know I want a female next time but I am thrilled that I will be a grandmother finally!"

Your mother is thrilled, I let them know.

She would prefer female younglings, I am sure. Tan's smugness is coming through loud and clear.

She did say something of the sort, I confirm. Then to Teyana, "You will have to wait a while for that female child. Let me get used to mothering twin boys."

Michelle looks at me with startled look. "How do you know they're males?"

"My mate, Akkadianans only birth male twins. Females are always singles," responds the big alien.

"I have not agreed to mate with you. Please quit calling me that." I feel she is protesting a bit much, but I understand the weirdness of the situation. I look at the big guy.

"So, do you have mating marks?" I ask. "You know that humans need to be courted, right?"

"I do have the marks," he states, "But I do not know of this courting business."

"Well, no girl wants to just a biological urge," I tell him like it is a big secret. "You are going to want to let her know that she is special to you." He gets this shocked look on his face; Michelle smirks.

"She is special. The gods have blessed me with a fated mate," he states emphatically. "Shu'baks see that as the ultimate privilege in our lives and she is my mate."

"Not if I don't wanna be, big guy!" Michelle yells at him.

Another dumb alien falls for a human, I think. *They just don't learn.*

I don't think we are dumb, just blessed by a Universe that knew what we needed, Tan says.

What we needed was a bit of chaos, Tet adds.

I love these guys, even if they are a bit stuffy. But not too stuffy.

Epilogue – Tet

"No Mother, Kelsey is doing fine." I look at my com and swear she thinks Tan and I can not take care of our mate. "She hasn't called you today because she is still sleeping.

"Oh, you two are hiding her away from me." My mother is very protective of her new daughter.

"Mother, we are not hiding her away," I assure her. "How an amazing scientist like you can be so irrational? Do our fathers approve of your hovering ways?"

"Of course not, darling," she chuckles. "They are like you and your brothers, all stoic. But I am like a youngling waiting for a special toy."

"Our sons are not toys, Mother." I have learned to roll my eyes like Kelsey.

Mother will not stop, Tet, says Tan, *it is not in her nature.* I agree with my brother then continue the conversation.

"Mother, we will have Kelsey call you when she wakes up." I tell her and end the call. I will not tolerate further silliness from my mother.

I think she is sweet, not silly, Kelsey sends to me.

Then you com her and deal with her annoying behavior, I tell my mate. *You talk to her everyday. What can you possibly discuss, my heart?*

We talk about raising babies and what naughty younglings you both were, she says.

We were perfect younglings, I defend. *We followed our fathers' teachings.*

And ignored your mother when she told you to behave? She states. Suddenly, Tan and I are running to our quarters, as we feel our mate cry out in pain. *Guys, I think this is it,* She tells us. *I will just com Michelle as I waddle to the Medic Clinic.*

You need to stay there until we get to you, my heart, I try to calm her. *We are on our way.*

I com the Medic Clinic and let them know we are on our way. They offer to send a bed and a medic to our quarters to help trans them. I tell them that she is safe with us and we will be there soon enough.

Are you sure about this? Tan jogs beside me.

Yes, I believe so, I state, though he can feel my nervousness. *We just need to get there in a few moments and take her to the clinic. She will be with medics in no time at all.*

As we walk into the room we hear our mate panting and moaning. She is standing beside the bed with wet towels under her.

Come, my heart. Let us get you to the clinic, Tan tries to reassure her but we can tell that she is in considerable pain.

"Fuck that! The first baby is coming," she screams at us.

No, my heart. The youngling will not come until we are at the clinic. It is that moment that I feel my son trying to push his way out of my beloved mate.

"You better get your ass over here and catch!" she screams, as Tan and I scramble to support her. I get next to her and take a peak between her legs. Yep, there is the crown of a head stretching her perfect vulva.

Tan, com the medics, this baby is almost here! I am frantic. One of our sons is ready to be born and there isn't a medic here nor the proper medical equipment. Trying not to panic, Tan and I try to support our mate holding her up as she squats over the towels. We grabbed up the wet ones and replaced them with clean and dry towels as quickly as possible.

The medic on the com tells us one of us will have to assist Kelsey in pushing out the youngling. Following the medic's instructions, Tan climbs on the bed and I lift our mate into his waiting arms. Mother had said that anything Kelsey says in labor is to be disregarded. I must do this because the things she is threatening to do to Tan and I sound very uncomfortable. Meanwhile, I am between her legs trying to guide our son out of our mate. It looks so painful.

"It fucking is painful you ASSHOLE!!!" At that moment, I am afraid of my mate. I have battled some of the fiercest pirates and criminals in the Universe yet I am so weakened by her. She is so strong and I am so pitiful as I wait to help.

"Breathe, my heart," I encourage her and let her know that the youngling is pushing his way out. I gently grab his head with both hands as it is emerging. Working to support his neck. "Push again, that is it!" His tiny shoulders follow after his head and as I gently pull the rest of his body emerges. I lay him in Kelsey's arms when I hear the chime of our quarters. Bidding the medics to come in, Kelsey's friend, Michelle, runs in and stops.

"I guess this little guy didn't want to wait to meet his mama," she says, gently moving me to Kelsey's side, as she examines my mate. "Now, Papas, you two still have work to do. Tet, hold the youngling while I cut the umbilical cord." She is swift and efficient with the laser that cuts and seals the cord, separating my youngling from my mate. I am in awe as I watch my son let out a cry so loud.

He is as loud as you, brother. Tet is amused by the cry yet also in awe of our son. We stop smiling when Kelsey's pain once again wracks her body. This time Michelle is there to assist our second son from Kelsey's ravaged body.

My heart, you are perfect, I say. *You are so strong.*

"Quit with the motivational poster sayings, Asshole!" Kelsey screams as she pushes one more time and our second youngling shows himself to the world. Again, Michelle cleans him up, handing this one to Kelsey and Tan. I join them and marvel at our happy family.

Michelle suddenly shouts, "Oh fuck there is another one!" and Kelsey's pain starts again.

Tan is in shock. *How did they not know there were three?*

Within a few minutes, Kelsey delivers the third youngling. A female. Tan and I are in awe. Akkadianans do not have three at a time. "Humans call them triplets," Kelsey says. "I forgot to tell you that multiples run in my family."

Multiples run in your family? I am amazed. Tan and I look at our daughter. So precious. We have two sons AND a daughter. Our mate is amazing!

Looking down at our family, life is so perfect for us. Mother will be thrilled. However, I think we will wait to tell her that Kelsey gave us triplets. For now, it is time for our beautiful family to rest.

The End.

Author's Note

Thank you for reading And Kelsey Makes Three. I hope you enjoyed my spicy little book. I will be continuing the story of our human woman who have found themselves in a strange situation of being the victims of alien abductors.

The next book is Yaritzi's Alien Prize. Read on to get a sneak peak at this new story. Yaritzi is an American of Mexican descent living in the Barrio Logan neighborhood of San Diego when she is abducted. From reading this book we have an idea of what happens to her. Kind of… There is a lot of issues for this human and her mate. So I hope this excerpt wets your whistle for Yaritzi's Alien Prize.

Sneak Peak

Yaritzi's Alien Prize

Chapter One – Yaretzi

My family thinks I'm odd. Though I am proud of my Mexican heritage, and I love living in San Ysidro on the California border with Mexico, I love studying the stars, planets, and galaxies! Abuela and Tia Lucinda like to look at each other as they pronounce that I will not find a husband if I keep my head in las Estrellas…the stars. I have family on both sides of that border and the family is a mix of modern American and traditional Mexican. I had both a quinceañera and a sweet sixteen. My parents raised us in Barrio Logan, but hoped we would one day make our way to living in La Jolla or North Park. Or, maybe, have homes on Coronado. They dreamed big for us. My older brother did move out to Spring Valley with his wife and my sister married a contractor from Ramona. So, they did pretty well for themselves. I just want to look at the stars. Someday, I want to finish my degree in astronomy and become a teacher, but, for now, I go to San Diego City College when I have the money. For now, I am a tow truck dispatcher for Garcia's Towing. This gives me the time and money to be able to come to Palomar Mountain's observatory. It isn't easy to get observer time because I am not a Caltech student. But they have gotten to know me at their viewing events and know that I am serious in my love of astronomy. My time was up, so I thought I would do a little hiking in the hills and do a little dreaming and stargazing and that is where they got me… The aliens…They had some cajónes abducting me near an observatory. They must've had some super stealth technology. All I remember is sitting on a rock overlooking the Palomar Mountains, just trying to do some gazing as the constellation Orion chased the Pleiades, just like the myth. Scorpio wasn't up yet. Yeah, that whole myth is fun. Zeus really is an ass in those stories, protecting his buddies, but Luna had none of it and set her scorpions against the sexual harassing Orion. Having to deal with entitled jerks like that most of my adult life, I really love the goddess Luna. I had her tattooed on my inner thigh. Yeah, the only man who sees her better feel blessed. So, anyway, I was just sitting there when I felt a prick on my neck. I turned quickly enough to see the weird, pale, nerdy guy before I passed out. When I woke up I was in a cage. An okay cage, decent bed, and a restroom…sort of…but still a cage. I wasn't awake long. I did have a few minutes to meet some of the women around me, Millie, and Kelsey, when the ship began shaking from the attack by our "rescuers". Yeah, Galactic Marines rescued us and now, they say we can't go home to Earth. We can't even leave this fucking starship because those aliens that abducted us have been kidnapping more humans…*pendejos*…My dad would say... OK, I say it too, but not in front of my parents. I should be thrilled that I am out among the stars, but I am not. I have a bit of claustrophobia on this ship and I just feel like I shouldn't be here. Not here in space but on this ship. I needed to get off this ship. That is when it happened. There was some kind of chemical leak in the ship, we not only had to dock but evacuate the ship. All of us humans had been herded into a large warehouse with several of the crew. Everyone just milling around. That is when Millie, Kelsey and I were up for an adventure and found a way to sneak off on to the station… While no one was looking, we snuck behind some shelves and then out a doorway into a hall. "We need to stick together and protect each other." Kelsey says, "Remember, we don't want to be captured by the bad guys. Just want to get a feel for this station. Maybe, do some shopping. We will charge it my mates!" "You are crazy," I tell her. She has two guys who have said she is their mate, but here she is risking the whole thing. I don't think she realizes what these military guys can be like. That is why I generally avoid them. Especially, the officers; total sticks up their butts. I hear the mate thing is forever, but I just don't see Kelsey working with these guys. The universe can be cruel. "Let's get going. We only have a few hours before they figure out that we are gone…That is if we are lucky." Millie nods, she never says much and always at whisper. I think that girl has had some serious troubles in her life. So, it surprised me that she wanted to come with us. We head out carefully into the empty hallway. Do we know where we were going? Oh, hell no we have no clue, but we are on an adventure. When we got to the end, we had to chose. "Which way?" I ask. "I don't know." Kelsey says. Millie reaches into the pocket of her pants and pulls out a quarter and hands it to me. "OK. Heads is to the right," I flip the coin, "It's tails." We head down the left hallway, looking for a door that might lead out into the main part of the station. I keep an ear out for crew members. We stopped at a few doorways, they either wouldn't open for us or we could hear alien voices on the other side. Luckily, the medic onboard the Patience had installed a translator on all of us, without it this would have been even more stupid idea than it is just on general principal. Three young women running around an alien space station without a clue of where we were going, knowing that there are alien bad guys snatching humans. What are we thinking? This isn't like going to TJ with my cousin Marisol to get drunk before we were 21. My parents were not happy. Though we weren't punished that hard because we had the sense to take a Trolley to the border and walk to the bars. Nah, we only had to listen to a lecture about how there are Mexican cartels that will take young girls to work the brothels in seedy areas of Tijuana or in Ensenada. I swear, they sounded like they were reciting something from a telenovela or a Trump rally. It was a bit of a letdown that I only saw sailors on leave from 32nd Street and North Island, pretty boring and the drinks were watered down…I knew not to tell my parents that! I liked my life a little too much to back talk. Being twenty-three, they were lenient. What were they gonna do? Ground me? But I still try to be respectful of their beliefs and "rules". That is why I didn't tell them when I got birth control prescribed when I turned eighteen, not that I needed it.. Even though they left the Church years ago, in favor of a Episcopal Church that preached the Gospel in Spanish and English and had a traditional liturgy without all the guilt, they still kept telling me that I didn't need to "kill babies" with birth control and I should just abstain from sex…yeah, that wasn't happening, if the right guy comes around… Victoria may buy all that virgin until marriage shit, I don't. Sex is part of a healthy human life…Marriage isn't as healthy. I have seen the black eyes on some of my friends when they had "fallen"….I just hadn't found a guy that floated my boat, not any moral need to stay chaste and pure keep slinking down this hallway, until we find a door that opens for us. Looking around, we see a lobby area and doors in front of us. There is a large desk area to the right with what looks to be an alien security guard…Wow, look at those tentacles… and straight ahead, was our goal, a door to the outside…well, not exactly the outside, as close as we are going to get on a space station "OK, we need to look like we are supposed to be here." I whisper. "Just keep walking with purpose. We will worry about getting back in when we are done." We begin to walk with purpose towards the door. Unfortunately, the tentacle guy notices us. "Hey, I don't think you three should be in here!" He, I assume he, is yelling at us. "Keep going, I will stall him." Whispering to my friends. I turn to him and say, "You are right!" I sashay over to him, not sure how the hip sway works with his species, but it worth a shot, "We aren't supposed to be here. We have a meeting in another part of the station, but our meeting here went overlong." I flutter my eyelashes and stick out my ample chest. His bulbous eyes look at my chest with interest tentacles sneak over the counter top with obvious intent. This allows Millie and Kelsey to leave the lobby, but I take a step back…Oh, no, mister, these are mine and you don't get to touch them… Tentacle guy's eyes narrow, as his advance is rebuffed. "Who are you and what are you doing here?" He says menacingly. I notice one of his tentacles has pressed the panel in front of him. "I told you, we were on our way out of a meeting." I blink with my best "ditzy" look. "With who?" Tentacles asks. "Who did you have meeting with?" I looked at the wall behind him and saw a name on a list with other important sounding people. "Well, it was with Mr. At…Ar..ith." "You mean Senior Councilor At'Arith?" He looks skeptical. "That's who I said!" I am not doing a good job of bluffing. Another guard walks into the lobby. He is a different species than the first. Big, grey and looking like a bulldog "Wollip, watch this female while I check with the Senior Councilor." …Well, that was a short excursion…I look wistfully out the windows in the front the lobby space. The view is amazing, if you didn't look up you would think you were looking at a small town square with what look like shops and restaurants. "Yes, sir. I will hold her here, sir."… Yep, my bid for freedom is over. Have fun girls, I am done…

Yaritzi's Alien Prize Look for it Summer of 2024!

About The Author

Viola Quincy currently lives in Northern Nevada with a cat, her husband and their almost adult child, Viola Quincy enjoys science fiction, romance and playing with string when she isn't writing spicy scenes and sexy aliens.

More Books by Viola Quincy

Alien's Songbird
Mommy's Big Alien

Join me online!

www.violaquincy.com

I am also on Facebook and make an appearance on TikTok every so often.

Made in the USA
Las Vegas, NV
27 January 2024

84944719R00114